# EUROPEAN MYTHS & TALES

## Carolyn Swift

**POOLBEG**

First published 1992 by
Poolbeg Press Ltd
Knocksedan House,
Swords, Co Dublin, Ireland

© Carolyn Swift, 1992

The moral right of the author has been asserted.

Poolbeg Press receives assistance from
The Arts Council / An Chomhairle Ealaíon, Ireland.

ISBN 1 85371 203 5

A catalogue record for this book is available from the British Library.

Cover design by Carol Betera
Set by Richard Parfrey in ITC Stone Serif 10/14pt
Printed by The Guernsey Press Company Ltd,
Vale, Guernsey, Channel Islands

## ABOUT THIS BOOK

Although these stories are called *European Myths and Tales*, the continent of Europe was divided very differently at the time these stories were written. There were many small kingdoms which today are no more than provinces and these were constantly being attacked and conquered by different races.

The Greek and Roman empires included many countries outside present-day Greece and Italy. The Celts, who came from the East, spread out over Western Europe, settling in areas such as Ireland, Scotland, Wales, Cornwall and Brittany. The Vikings sailed in their longships from Scandinavia, invading the coasts of countries all over Europe, including Ireland, Britain and even the north-west of Russia, so that the story about Thor, which was written down by an Icelander, would also have been told in many parts of Europe besides Norway, Sweden and Denmark.

For these reasons, stories told in the mythology of one country are often set in what is now a different nation. The tale of Gudrun, the captive princess, which is from the Teutonic (or German) branch of Nordic (or Viking) mythology, is about people living in present-day Belgium, the Netherlands and France, while the story of Beowulf, though it takes place in what is now Scandinavia, was written in Old English and is therefore one of the few surviving pieces of Anglo-Saxon mythology. Even Siegfried, who is the great hero-figure of German mythology, as

Cúchulainn is of the Irish, was a prince of the Netherlands, said to have been "born in the city of Xanten on the Rhine."

The story of Thor may seem the most puzzling of all, since it is set in the Land of the Gods and the Land of the Giants, but both of these places were very real to the Vikings. Yet, though they even had maps showing the exact locations of Asgard and Outgard, marking in the sea and the mountains, they were not placed anywhere in our world. So don't worry too much about the countries in which the stories are set. The important thing is that they are all tales that were told by people who lived somewhere in the place we now call Europe.

Carolyn Swift, 1992

# Contents

*For Lena*

*So she may read the tales of her English, French, Dutch and Italian ancestors, as well as those of her Irish grandfathers— and tales of many other Europeans too.*

# The Adventures of Perseus

Once upon a time there lived a boy named Perseus. He was brave, handsome and strong, but he was unlucky enough to stand in the way of the King of Seriphos, the small Greek island where he lived. The trouble was that the king had fallen in love with Perseus's mother and a devoted teenage son seemed to him to be a definite handicap in his pursuit of her.

The king thought of having Perseus killed, but he was popular with the people of Seriphos and the king was afraid they might rebel if they suspected dirty work. Then he hit on a plan that seemed to him to be foolproof.

Far away to the south-west lived three sisters known as the Gorgons. They had teeth like the tusks of a wild boar, every hair on their heads was a writhing snake and altogether they looked quite hideous. Their looks hardly mattered, though, because anyone who looked them in the face was immediately turned to stone. Two of the sisters could never be killed because they were immortal, but the third, Medusa, was mortal. Everyone who had tried to kill her, however, had been turned to stone before he could succeed. That, thought the king, would be a splendid way of getting Perseus out of his way for good.

When Perseus asked the king what he wanted for his birthday, therefore, the king gave his answer at once.

"More than anything in the world," he said, "I would

like the head of Medusa."

Now when a king asks for a particular present, no one can ask him if he wouldn't be just as happy with a nice book. Besides, Perseus was a brave boy and eager to prove himself a fine warrior, so he set sail at once for the southwest.

After many days his ship washed up on the shores of a country very different from his rocky Greek island. All he could see was miles and miles of sand, sparkling under the hot sun till his eyes ached, but he walked and walked, feeling thirstier and thirstier, until he saw some palm trees in the distance. Knowing that where there were trees there should be water, he hurried towards them and found, beside them, a wooden hut. Hoping for food and directions to the place Medusa lived, he knocked on the door.

"Come in!" replied a cracked, quavering voice, so in he went.

Inside there were three old hags, huddled on the hut floor, and when they turned towards him he saw that the first had only one eye and no teeth, the second only one tooth and no eyes, while the third had neither eyes nor teeth.

"I am a traveller," Perseus said uneasily, "and I would be grateful for a little food and water and directions for my journey."

"You're very young to be wandering around Africa by yourself," snarled the hag with the one eye, suspiciously. "What do you think, sisters? Should we help him?"

"I can't say without seeing him first," croaked the hag with the one tooth. "Pass me the eye!"

To Perseus's amazement, the first hag took out her eye and gave it to the second hag, who wiped it on her apron and put it into her own face as casually as if she were putting on glasses.

"He looks all right to me," she croaked, after staring at Perseus with the eye. "He can share our supper. Bring it right away, sister."

"How can I," wavered the hag with neither tooth nor eye, "when I can't see to get it? Pass me the eye!"

Perseus tried not to stare while the second hag took out the eye and passed it to the third, who didn't even bother wiping it before pushing it into her own face. After a glance at Perseus, she hobbled about, preparing a meal. Looking round the hut while she did so, Perseus was surprised to see a helmet sitting on a shelf beside a sling bag. The helmet seemed a very war-like thing for these old women to own, especially as there was nothing else there but a few simple plates, bowls, cups and jars made of pottery.

"That's a fine helmet," he said politely, "even though it's dull and black instead of shiny and silver."

"Aha!" smirked the first hag. "There's a reason why it's black."

"There is indeed," croaked the second hag, "for that makes it invisible."

"Better still," quavered the third, as she set a jug of water in front of him, "anyone who wears it becomes invisible too."

Perseus thought that being invisible might be a great help in trying to kill Medusa, but he kept his thoughts to himself. Instead he asked how he would find the Gorgons.

"That's a secret!" snarled the first hag.

"And one you would be better not knowing," croaked the second, "for if you find them you will only end up a stone statue, like all the others."

"So eat, drink and rest," quavered the third, as she set in front of him a dish of beans and another of dates. "Then you can go back where you came from and be thankful you are still alive."

Perseus argued with them but it was no use. Anyway, they could now think of nothing but eating, which was both slow and difficult for them, as they had to pass the one tooth backwards and forwards between them, as they had done earlier with the one eye. When their hunger was satisfied, they put the eye and the tooth into a box and settled down for a nap.

Now, Perseus thought, even if they wake they won't be able to see me, so he tiptoed over to the helmet and tried it on. It fitted perfectly. It struck him then that he would need something to put Medusa's head in after he had cut it off, so he took the sling bag as well. He felt guilty about stealing from the three sisters when they had given him supper, but he told himself he must take every opportunity if he were to succeed in his almost impossible task. All he needed now was to find the way to Medusa's home. The three sisters obviously knew, if only he could make them tell him. Then his eye fell on the box. Without an eye or a tooth between them they would be lost, he thought.

"Wake up!" he cried, snatching up the box, "and tell me how I may find Medusa."

"That we will never do," snarled the first hag, "so be quiet and let us sleep in peace!"

"Then I'm afraid you'll starve!" cried Perseus, "for I have your eye and tooth. Without them you won't be able to look for food nor eat it when you have it."

At once the three began to wail, begging Perseus to return the box.

"Gladly," Perseus told them, "as soon as you tell me

the way I must go."

"Then your death will be on your own head," croaked the second hag. "Go west across Africa till you reach the sea on the further side. There you will find a palace and, beside it, a garden with golden apples hanging from the trees. The gate is guarded by a dragon and it will be your own fault when he kills you!"

"But what about Medusa?" asked Perseus.

"If by a miracle you escape the dragon," the third hag quavered, "go through the garden till you come to a great lake. There you will find Medusa and it will be your own fault when she turns you to stone!"

"Thank you," said Perseus. "Here is your eye and your tooth."

And placing the box in the first hag's hand, he ran out of the door with the helmet and the sling bag before she could put the eye into her head.

For days he travelled across the desert until he came to a land where crops grew. There he saw a magnificent palace beside a beautiful garden with high walls and, just as the second hag had told him, a dragon with glaring eyes and fiery breath sat at the gate. Perseus put on the black helmet and edged nervously past the dragon, but he never moved, so Perseus went boldly in through the garden gate and walked on until he came to the lake.

He was about to take off his helmet to drink when he heard a roaring sound and felt a great rush of wind beside him. Turning, he found to his horror a mass of writhing snakes at the water's edge. He trembled as he realised he was looking at the back of Medusa's head, as she too stooped to drink from the lake. He knew his helmet made him invisible, but even so he was terrified that she might turn her head towards him so that he would find himself looking into her face and be turned to stone.

The snakes held his gaze with a horrible fascination, but he forced himself to turn away. As he did so, he suddenly saw the head reflected in his shield, which was polished so brightly that it sparkled like a mirror. Then Perseus had an idea. Keeping his eyes on the shield so he could use the reflection to guide his hand, he raised his sword and struck off Medusa's head without ever turning back to face her. Then he thrust the head into the bag which was slung around his neck.

Now he knew it would be safe to inspect the ugly, scaly body and talon-like claws but, before he could do more than glance at them, he again heard the great rushing wind and saw two more scaly creatures with outstretched talons, flying towards the body of Medusa. In a flash he guessed it must be the other two Gorgon sisters.

Even though he was invisible, Perseus thought in sudden panic, they would see the top of Medusa's head sticking out of his bag and hurry to avenge their sister's death. How could he escape? He sprang to his feet, snatched up his sword and, as he did so, a drop of Medusa's blood fell from it to the ground. Instantly, to his amazement, a winged horse sprang up in its place. Without stopping to think, Perseus leaped on to its back as it rose into the air, carrying him swiftly back the way he had come.

After a while, Pegasus—for that was the name of the winged horse—landed in a city on the edge of the desert and Perseus noticed all the people in the streets were weeping. Pushing his way through them to the palace, he asked the sobbing servant if the king was dead.

"No," the servant told him between sobs, "King Cepheus is not dead, but his daughter Andromeda soon will be. The oracle foretold that only her death could save our people from being devoured one by one by the terrible sea-monster that has ravaged our kingdom for years. At this very moment, she is chained to a rock on the seashore, waiting for the monster to claim her."

"Then I must save her," Perseus cried, racing towards the sea.

There he saw a girl with long golden hair blowing about her shoulders as the waves rose about her waist. Just as he reached her, a great black slimy tentacle came out of the sea and gripped her. Snatching up his sword, Perseus hacked the tentacle off but immediately another replaced it, this time circling his body and crushing it in a vice-like grip.

Perseus struggled as never before but, no matter how many tentacles he cut off, the monster always seemed to have more. He felt himself being dragged down and then a huge bloated head appeared, the great jaws gaping wide to swallow him. Desperately, he thrust his sword down its mouth and felt its grip on him relax. Its slimy black body was floating away lifeless on the waves. Hurrying to untie Andromeda from her rock, Perseus thought her the most beautiful girl he had ever seen.

"How can I ever thank you?" cried the delighted king, when Perseus brought back his daughter. "Whatever you ask shall be yours."

Glancing at Andromeda, standing beside him and looking at him with big, adoring eyes, Perseus suddenly knew exactly what he wanted.

"I would like Andromeda to be my wife," he said boldly.

"And I would gladly give her to you," the king replied, "but she is engaged to Prince Phineus, whose country borders ours. He is very proud and would never allow another to take her."

"He didn't do much to stop the sea-monster from taking her," Perseus argued, and the whole court cheered, for they hated the haughty Phineus.

"That's true," the king agreed. "Then you shall have her, but Phineus may make trouble when he hears about it."

"Let him!" cried Perseus. "We will be married as soon as arrangements can be made, if Andromeda is willing."

Andromeda nodded eagerly, for she much preferred her gallant rescuer to the cold prince, rich and powerful though he was. So the wedding was arranged and a great feast held to celebrate it. Suddenly one of the king's soldiers hurried in to say the look-out had sighted Phineus, advancing on the palace at the head of a large army. There was panic all round, but Perseus remained calm.

"Do as I say and all will be well," he cried. "Bring me my sling bag!"

A servant hurried to obey him and, when he had brought the bag, Perseus told everyone to close their eyes. Then, carefully taking out the head of Medusa so that its back was towards him, he held it aloft and stood waiting.

When Phineus and his army marched in, the first thing they saw was the face of Medusa and immediately they were all turned to stone. So Perseus married the beautiful Andromeda and there was great rejoicing in the land. One day, however, Perseus told Andromeda that it was time for him to return to Seriphos.

"My mother will be worried about me," he said. "Anyway, it's high time that she met you. And I have to give the head of Medusa to the king. He should be really impressed for I'm sure he never thought I'd manage to get it."

So they said goodbye to King Cepheus and set sail for Seriphos. When they dropped anchor in the little harbour, Perseus asked Andromeda if she would mind waiting on board ship for a while.

"Just till I've broken it to my mother that I'm married," he explained. "She might get a shock if we just walked into the palace together."

So he set off on his own. As he passed the Temple of Minerva, however, he saw a large, excited crowd and, pushing his way through to the great door of the temple, found his mother clinging to the altar and crying on the goddess Minerva to protect her. Then Perseus saw the king, surrounded by his guards.

"What's wrong, mother?" he called.

"Oh, thanks be to Minerva you're back!" she cried. "As soon as you left, the king began pestering me to marry him. No matter how many times I refused him he kept insisting and now he has ordered his guards to take me by force."

"Seize him too!" shouted the king to his guards. "He shall die for his interference!"

The guards hurried towards Perseus, but he turned to face the king.

"Wait!" he cried. "You asked for the head of Medusa and I've brought it to you!"

Then Perseus held the head high above his own, as he had done with Phineus, and immediately the king and his guards were all turned to stone. Then Perseus thrust the head back into its bag and embraced his mother. She was delighted to hear of his marriage and hurried to the ship to welcome her daughter-in-law, while the people rejoiced that they were rid of the cruel king.

"Now Perseus must be our king," they cried, "and if enemies attack us he can turn them all to stone!"

But Perseus decided that Medusa's head was far too dangerous for any mortal to have around the place, so he gave it to the warrior goddess Athena to put in the centre of her shield, and it has been there ever since.

♥♥♥

# The Orphans Who
# Founded a City

Long ago in the land that is now called Italy, there lived a beautiful princess named Rhea Silvia. She was the daughter of the King of Alba, but she never wore fine clothes or went to state banquets. Instead, she spent her days in the temple of the goddess Vesta for, when she was only seven, she had become one of the two priestesses whose chief job it was to make sure the sacred fire which burned before the statue of the goddess never went out.

It was thought a great honour to be a Vestal Virgin, as these priestesses were called, and only girls of royal birth were chosen. They had to take vows to stay away from men until they had served the goddess for thirty years, after which they could marry if they wished.

Vesta was the special goddess of mothers and on the seventh of June every year there was a festival when all mothers of families for miles around would go to the temple with gifts for the goddess, though at all other times, no one but the Vestal Virgins were allowed to enter it. Rhea Silvia and her companion would be very busy all that day with the religious ceremonies but, during the rest of the year, serving the goddess and keeping the temple in order was not a hard job and she was proud to have been chosen for it.

When Rhea Silvia was seventeen, however, her beauty was noticed by the Roman god, Mars. He was the god of war and, because there were a great many battles in those days, he was prayed to a great deal. Winning battles meant gaining both honour and riches, while losing them meant either being killed or having everything you owned taken from you by the conquerors, so it's not surprising that more prayers were said to Mars than even to Jupiter, who was the father of all the Roman gods. So Mars felt he had the right to anything he wanted and he quickly decided that he wanted Rhea Silvia. He knew, however, that she would not be allowed to break her vows even for a god and he had no intention of waiting for twenty years. Instead he waited until the night of the seventh of June, when he knew Rhea Silvia would be so exhausted from all the prayers she had offered for the goddess's feast day and all the plates of fruit and loaves of bread she had received from the mothers that nothing would wake her. Then he slipped secretly into the temple.

Months later, when Rhea Silvia became the mother of boy twins, everyone was very angry.

"You broke your vows," they all cried, "and the punishment for that is death."

"But I didn't!" protested Rhea Silvia. "I never kept company with any man! One of the gods gave me these babies!"

But of course no one believed her.

"Even if I must die, please spare my sons!" Rhea Silvia begged. "I will go peacefully to my tomb if they are allowed to live. Grant me this last wish, for I swear I never broke my vows and Vesta herself will surely punish you if you injure these innocent babies."

So, in the end, everyone swore by Vesta not to kill the boys, though the strict laws of the time meant that Rhea Silvia herself had to die and she went proudly to her death, declaring her innocence to the end. Then everyone began to argue about what to do with the twins.

"We can't possibly rear them," said one man. "The children of a Vestal Virgin! It would be a terrible scandal!"

"But we can't kill them," cried another. "We swore by Vesta that we wouldn't."

"Then there's only one thing to be done," said a wise woman. "Let us leave the matter to Vesta."

"And how do we do that?" asked the first man.

"Place them in the grain basket," the woman told him, "and set it afloat on the River Tiber. If Vesta wishes them to live, she will guide the basket to safety. If not, they will die. That way we will neither break our promise nor give scandal to the world."

Everyone was delighted at this solution and soon the day-old babies were gurgling with delight as the basket was rocked to and fro by the current on its way downstream. The goddess Vesta must indeed have wished to save the twins, because she caused the river to flood, so that the basket was washed ashore under a fig tree in front of the Temple of Lupercus. By now it was evening and the babies were trying to suck their thumbs and crying with hunger, but Vesta must have taken a hand in the matter once again since she was, after all, the goddess of mothers. A grey wolf crept down from the hills and fed the boys with her own milk, so they slept soundly that night.

It surely must have been luck, however, that the very next day was the fifteenth of February, which happened to be the Feast of Lupercal. That was when women who wanted to have children came to the Temple of Lupercus to pray for a baby and so it was that Acca Laurentia came early that morning, for she and her husband, Faustulus, the shepherd, had been married a long time and still had no children. She prayed for a long time and then walked down to the river to pick a fig from the fig tree. When she saw the basket hidden beneath it with the two baby boys sleeping peacefully, she cried out in delight.

"Thanks be to Lupercus, for he has given me not one son, but two!"

Then she carried the basket home to show her husband, who was as delighted with her find as she was herself. So the twins were reared as if they were the shepherd's own sons.

They lived in a simple herdsman's cottage high on the hillside, took their turn at minding the sheep and the goats and lived mainly on fresh goat's milk, cheese and bread baked by their foster mother, along with the fruit, nuts and herbs they gathered in the woods and on the grassy hillside below their home. They had no idea that their grandfather was a king, still less that they owed their birth to a god and that their lives had been saved by a goddess. Yet they had strange ideas for simple shepherd lads.

Each time they looked down on the River Tiber, winding its way around the foot of the hill with the cluster of temples beside it; at the grand houses grouped around the forum with its market stalls, and at the hovels of the poorer people sprawled along the river bank beyond, they dreamed of founding a great city.

"It would have high walls all round it to keep out invaders," said the twin who was called Romulus, "with several great gates in them with guard houses for the soldiers defending them."

"And all the temples and houses already built would be inside the walls," suggested the twin who was called

Remus, "only we would make them even bigger and grander. And maybe build extra temples to some of the other gods."

"And it would have fountains to make the air cool in summer and city baths where the people could bathe in hot and cold water," cried Romulus.

"And it would have a stadium for horse-racing and all contests of strength and speed and skill," enthused Remus.

"And a fine library where people could go to read what the wise men have written," Romulus shouted in excitement.

"And a theatre and a concert hall," added Remus, not to be outdone. "And we can make the forum bigger so there is room to bring more goods into the city for selling."

"And the city will be in the shape of a square," finished Romulus.

So, day after day, while they minded the sheep, they added to their imaginary city, planning marble streets and a hotel for rich guests and a dungeon for people who broke the laws and a proper harbour on the river bank and schools for boys and girls and, of course, a grand city hall where the laws of the city would be made. As they grew to manhood, they talked so much about their city that their foster father went to see the augur. He was the man the king paid to foretell the future and, to Faustulus's amazement, he told him that the gods had ordained that the twins should found a city.

"They are to watch the skies for a sign," he told him. "Romulus is to watch the heavens to the north and Remus the heavens to the south. Let them take special note of the flight of birds."

So from then on, while the boys minded the sheep,

they watched the skies too. One day, six vultures appeared in the southern half of the sky.

"It must be the sign," cried Remus. "Never before have I seen six vultures together when there was no dead lamb to attract them."

But, at that very moment, Romulus saw there were twelve vultures in his half of the sky.

"No, that is the sign," he shouted in triumph, "and the city shall be called after me."

Racing off, he borrowed a plough from the farmer at the foot of the hill, took a white cow and a white bull which were grazing nearby and must surely have been placed there by the gods for the purpose, since he had never seen them there before, and harnessed them to the plough. Then he ploughed a furrow in a great square around the temples, houses and forum, to mark out where the city walls would be built.

"That shall be the boundary of the great city," he shouted to Remus.

"What, this shallow trench?" sneered Remus, scuffing his way across it and breaking the line left by the plough. "A few stray goats grazing across it will wipe it out overnight. Besides, it's in the wrong place!"

"Will you destroy my city as you have destroyed my plan?" roared Romulus in rage, hitting Remus on the head.

Remus fell to the ground, striking his head on the plough shaft, and lay still. Bending over him, Romulus realised that he was dead. He tried to forget his feelings of guilt and distress, telling himself that Remus had tried to go against the design of the gods and so had to die. Then he set to work like a madman, to complete his plan. By the year 753 BC, the city was built and called Rome after

Romulus, just as he had dreamed.

One day, however, his foster mother told him that the ghost of his dead brother had appeared to her.

"His spirit cannot rest in peace," she told Romulus, "because you alone have been credited with planning the city. He says the gods will not forgive you if you allow his name to be forgotten."

Romulus was ashamed then and told the people how he and his brother had planned the city together. Then he set aside three days in May every year for Romans to honour the memory of Remus.

Today Rome is still one of the oldest and greatest cities in the world and Romulus must have been forgiven for his crime for, when he died, Mars came for him and took him up to heaven in a fiery chariot.

❧❧❧

# The Rescue of Mabon

A t the court of King Arthur, there was a young man named Gwrhyr who could speak every language in the world. Not only did he know the tongues of the Gaels, the Gauls, the Picts, the Scots, the Saxons, the Jutes and the Romans, but also the languages of every bird and beast, so Arthur made him his royal interpreter. One day, Arthur sent for him and when he arrived at the Council Chamber with its famous round table, he found that Kay, Arthur's foster brother, was there also.

"I've summoned you," Arthur told him, "because I'm sending Kay on a most important mission. When I captured the sword Excalibur (which means Hard Lightning) from the fortress of Kaer Sidhi last year, I would have perished with all my men if Modron the Birdwoman had not shown me how to escape the forces of Odgar. As a reward, I promised I would find her son Mabon, who has been missing for fourteen years. Now I've asked Kay to help me fulfil my promise."

"If I am to find him, I must first know how he disappeared," Kay said.

"That will not help in your search," Arthur replied, "for he was kidnapped as a baby. He was only three days old when he disappeared from his cot and no one ever found out who took him or why."

"In that case," Kay answered, "it would puzzle any

man to know where to begin the search."

"That's why I'm sending my interpreter with you," Arthur told him, "for he'll be able to question the birds of the air and the beasts of the forest. Sooner or later you'll surely find one who has seen or heard something."

So Kay and Gwrhyr set off on their travels. After a while, they came to Cilgwri and there, sitting on the branch of a tree, they found the Blackbird.

"The Blackbird of Cilgwri is said to be a wise old bird," Kay said to Gwrhyr. "Ask him if he knows where we may find Mabon, son of Modron."

So Gwrhyr repeated the question in bird-language and the Blackbird tilted his head to one side and thought about it for a long time.

"When I first came to Cilgwri," he said finally, "I was only a young bird. In those days there was a smith working here, beating his horseshoes into shape on that anvil you see there. The smith has been dead for a long time now and no one uses the anvil except me, for I crack my nuts open upon it with my beak. The anvil is almost worn out from my battering and yet, in all that long time, I've never heard a word of Mabon, son of Modron."

"Then we'll have to ask someone else," Gwrhyr said.

"I'll tell you what I'll do," the Blackbird told him. "Since I respect Arthur and you come as his messenger, I'll take you to someone who is older than I am. Maybe he will know."

So the Blackbird flew off through the forest and Kay and Gwrhyr followed him between the tree trunks. After a while, they came to Rhedynfrc and there, grazing in a clearing, they found the Stag.

"The Stag of Rhedynfrc is said to be even older and wiser than the Blackbird of Cilgwri," said Kay. "Ask him if he knows where we may find Mabon, son of Modron."

So Gwrhyr repeated the question in deer-language and the Stag rubbed his antlers against a tree stump and thought about it for a long time.

"When I first came to Rhedynfrc," he said finally, "I had only a small spike of antler beginning to grow on each side of my head. Now I've such huge, branched antlers that I cannot pass close to a tree for fear of becoming tangled in it. And what was only a young sapling when I first came here grew into a mighty oak tree with a hundred branches and then became so old that it fell in last winter's storms. All that's left of it now is that stump you see there and yet, in all that long time, I never heard a word of Mabon, son of Modron."

"Then we'll have to ask someone else," Gwrhyr said.

"I'll tell you what I'll do," the Stag told him. "Since I respect Arthur and you come as his messenger, I'll take you to someone who is even older than I am. Maybe he will know."

So the Stag set off through the forest and Kay and Gwrhyr followed him until they came to Cwm Cawlwyd and there, on an ivy-covered stump at the edge of the forest, they found the Owl.

"The Owl of Cwm Cawlwyd is said to be even older and wiser than the Stag of Rhedynfrc," said Kay. "Ask him if he knows where we may find Mabon, son of Modron."

So Gwrhyr repeated the question in owl-language and the Owl blinked at them and thought about it for a long time.

"When I first came to Cwm Cawlwyd," he said finally, "it was a great forest, but men came and, in their carelessness, burned it down. Then a second forest grew up but other men came and chopped it down to build ships for their warriors to invade other lands. This forest you have just travelled through is the third to grow in the same valley and yet, in all that long time, I never heard a word of Mabon, son of Modron."

"Then we'll have to ask someone else," Gwrhyr said.

"I'll tell you what I'll do," the Owl told him. "Since I respect Arthur and you come as his messenger, I'll take you to someone who is even older than I am. Maybe he will know."

So the Owl flew away towards the mountains and Kay and Gwrhyr followed him across the valley and up a steep rocky track. After a while they came to Gwernabwy and there, perched on a crag, they found the Eagle.

"The Eagle of Gwernabwy is said to be even older and wiser than the Owl of Cwm Cawlwyd," said Kay. "Ask him if he knows where we may find Mabon, son of Modron."

So Gwrhyr repeated the question in eagle-language and the Eagle preened his feathers and thought about it for a long time.

"When I first came to Gwernabwy," he said finally, "there was a rock so high that it seemed to me I could peck at the stars if I could only stand on top of it. Now I can sharpen my beak on its summit without even stretching my neck. I've travelled from the sea in the north to the sea in the south and from the sea in the east to the sea in the west, but in all that long time and in all that distance I never heard a word of Mabon, son of Modron."

"Then we'll have to ask someone else," Gwrhyr said.

"I'll tell you what I'll do," the Eagle told him. "Since I respect Arthur and you come as his messenger, I'll take you to someone who is even older than I am and who has travelled even further. Maybe he will know."

So the Eagle flew off and Kay and Gwrhyr hurried down the mountainside and across the valley after him until they came upon him perched on a cliff above the waters of Llyn Llyw.

"One day," he said to them when they came close enough to hear, "I came to this place in search of food and saw a great salmon leaping. I sank my claws into him to carry him away but he was so strong he dragged me down into the water with him as he dived and I'd have been drowned if I hadn't let go of him. Later we made our peace and he told me how every year he travelled the oceans of the world before returning to this pool. Now I'll call him, for if he has not heard of the man you seek, I fear there is no one who can help you."

Then the Eagle flew on to a rock in the middle of the water and called: "Salmon of Llyn Llyw, oldest, wisest and most travelled of all creatures, will you help these messengers of Arthur, wisest of mortals?"

Suddenly a great scaly head rose from the lake surface and the two men gasped to see, like a dark shadow beneath the water, a body almost as big as a grown man.

"What do they want, these messengers of Arthur?" asked the Salmon, in a voice that sounded like water thundering down the mountainside.

"They seek news of Mabon, son of Modron, who was taken from his mother when he was only three days old," the Eagle told him.

The Salmon flicked his fins so that they shone and sparkled like silver in the sunlight and thought about it for a long time.

"With every tide," he said finally, "I swim upstream as far as the great stone fortress of Caer Loyw and from inside its walls I hear such wailing and moaning that it would break your heart. I don't know if this prisoner is the man you seek but, if you wish to see for yourself, let one of you stand on each of my shoulders and I will carry you there."

So Kay and Gwrhyr climbed on to the shoulders of the great Salmon, while the Eagle flew overhead, and they all went upstream until they came to a high wall rising steeply from beside the river bank. Far above they could see a small window with heavy bars across it and from this came a terrible moaning, just as the Salmon had described.

"Who weeps so piteously inside this bleak prison?" called Kay, with his hands cupped on each side of his mouth.

Then they saw two hands grip the bars and a boy's head between them.

"It is I, Mabon son of Modron," his voice echoed down to them, "and no one has been treated so unjustly or so cruelly."

"Will gold or silver buy your freedom?" Kay cried back to him.

"No!" came his reply, sad and despairing. "Only the defeat of my captors will release me."

"Do not despair," Kay called again, "for Arthur has sent us to find you and, as soon as he learns where you are, he'll summon his best warriors to rescue you."

So Kay and Gwrhyr returned to the court and told Arthur what they had discovered. Then Arthur rode to Caer Loyw at the head of a great body of men and attacked the fortress. The evil kidnappers and their men fought back, raining down stones and boiling oil from the battlements but, while they were all fighting at the front of the fortress, Kay and Gwrhyr rode on the shoulders of the Salmon as he swam upstream, with the Eagle flying above them, until they reached the back of the fortress once more.

Then the Eagle perched on the battlements and used his sharp beak to break through the bars of the cell, while Kay, Gwrhyr and the Salmon kept a look-out below. In a few minutes they saw Mabon, son of Modron, climb onto the Eagle's back and fly with him towards the mountains. Kay gave Arthur a signal and he and his men fought their way back out of the fortress, helped by Kay and Gwrhyr. Then they all returned to Caerleon, taking with them Mabon, son of Modron, free at last, thanks to the birds and the beasts of the forest and Gwrhyr's ability to speak to them in their own language.

# Gráinne

There was once a High King in Ireland called Cormac, who had a daughter as clever as she was beautiful, but she was also strong-willed and independent. Indeed, her father had learned to his cost that he could make no arrangements for her unless she agreed to them. That's why when Fionn MacCumhaill's son Oisín called to see the king to ask for her as bride for his widowed father, the king paled.

"There's hardly a prince or champion in Ireland that Gráinne hasn't already refused to marry," he cried, "and they all blame me for it and threaten war in revenge. I don't want Fionn of all people for an enemy, so please ask her yourself so you can tell him there's no one but Gráinne to blame when she refuses."

Then Cormac took Oisín to Gráinne's room and sat down beside her.

"This is the son of Fionn MacCumhaill, leader of the invincible Fianna," he told her, trying to suggest the need for a civil answer. "He wants you to agree to marry his father."

"If you'd like Fionn for a son-in-law I'm sure I'd like him well enough for a husband," Gráinne said politely.

Surprised and delighted, Cormac invited Fionn to meet Gráinne at a banquet in Tara, with all the Fianna, chiefs and nobles of Ireland. Fionn was seated on the king's right, while Gráinne sat on his left, with the king's chief druid on her other side, and she began asking him to name the members of the Fianna on Fionn's side of the table.

"Oisín I've met," she said, "but who is the graceful youth beside him?"

"That's Oscar, Oisín's son and Fionn's grandson," he told her.

"And the haughty-looking man beside him?"

"That's Fionn's nephew."

"And the handsome man with the black curly hair and freckles, who talks so vivaciously and has such a lovely smile?"

"That's Diarmuid O Duibhne, whom all the women in Ireland dream about."

"I see," Gráinne said thoughtfully and then, turning to look at Fionn, added: "It's strange Fionn doesn't want me for a daughter-in-law rather than a wife, when he's even older than my father."

"Hush," cried the druid, shocked, "for if Fionn hears you he'll neither marry you himself nor let anyone belonging to him do so."

Then Gráinne called her servant to bring her great gold goblet, which held enough for twenty men, and filled it to the brim.

"Take this to Fionn," she ordered, "and say I sent it so he may drink to our future."

Fionn raised the goblet to Gráinne and took a long drink from it. Then Gráinne offered it to her father, her mother, Eitche and her brother Cairbre and they also drank deeply from it, for it would have seemed rude not to in a toast to the engaged couple. Within minutes of drinking, however, Fionn, Cormac, Eitche and Cairbre had all fallen into a deep sleep. Then Gráinne went to Diarmuid O Duibhne and asked him to marry her in Fionn's place.

"Certainly not," Diarmuid replied, "for that would be to betray Fionn."

"Then I put you under *geasa* to take me away from here before Fionn wakes," Gráinne told him, "for I once saw you play hurley against my brother and from that day on I've looked at no man but you."

"Now what can I do," cried Diarmuid, "for it's shameful to betray Fionn, but even more shameful not to do something I've been bound to do under *geasa*?"

"You've no choice but to go with Gráinne," Oisín told him.

"That's true," agreed Oscar, "for you must obey a *geasa*, even though it leads to your death."

"Certainly," added Fionn's nephew, "and I'm only sorry it wasn't I this beautiful princess chose, but I warn you: watch out for Fionn, for he will never rest until he's had his revenge."

So Diarmuid said goodbye to his comrades and went with Gráinne. Taking two of the king's horses and a chariot, they drove all the way from Tara to Athlone that night, when the horses were too exhausted to go further.

"Leave them here," Gráinne said, "but to prevent Fionn tracing us, let's leave one on each side of the river and walk a mile upstream in the water so Fionn may not find our footprints."

Following this plan, they reached the western bank of the Shannon, crossing the border into Connacht at daybreak. There they hid in an oak-wood and, making a rough shelter of branches, finally dared to sleep.

Next morning, when Fionn found they had gone, he

was furious. He sent his best trackers to find them and, though they were delayed by Gráinne's plan to hide their footprints, in the end they reached the oak-wood and sent word to Fionn, who set out at once with his army. As he approached Athlone, Oscar secretly sent Fionn's hound Bran to warn Diarmuid but, despite Gráinne's pleading, Diarmuid wouldn't try to escape.

"We can't out-distance Fionn now," he said, "and I would rather face him than be captured trying to escape."

Then Oisín got Feargoir, who was famous for his loud voice, to shout a warning, but again Diarmuid wouldn't listen to Gráinne's pleas for him to run. Finally Aengus, son of the chief of the dé Danan, who had taught Diarmuid as a boy, decided to use his magic powers to rescue him. He flew on the wind from his home at Newgrange to the oak-wood and told Diarmuid and Gráinne they could escape under cover of his invisible cloak, but again Diarmuid refused.

"Take Gráinne," he told Aengus, "and if I'm not killed I'll follow you."

So Aengus hid Gráinne under his cloak and took her to Limerick. No sooner had they gone than Diarmuid heard the sound of Fionn's army approaching.

"Come out, Diarmuid," Fionn shouted, "for you are surrounded and cannot escape us."

Then Diarmuid took his longest spear and used it to pole-vault so high over the heads of Fionn's men that the tree tops were between them and they didn't even see him pass. Then he joined Aengus and Gráinne in Limerick and Gráinne was so relieved to see him she could hardly speak.

"I must go," Aengus told them, "but I warn you: keep moving, for Fionn will never give up. Put distance between the place where you cook your meal and where you eat it, and the place where you eat and where you sleep."

So Diarmuid and Gráinne fled to Kerry and, for months, travelled its forests, mountains and valleys, always keeping on the move. One day, on the slopes of Sliabh Luachra, they met two tall swordsmen.

"We are of the Clan Morna," they told him. "Both our fathers fought at the Battle of Castleknock, when Fionn's father was killed and, though they died before we were born, Fionn is demanding that we pay for his father's death."

"What payment does he expect?" Gráinne asked.

"He wants Diarmuid's head," said one.

"Or a fistful of berries from the tree of Dubros," added the other.

"I'm surprised you chose to trail us," Gráinne said, "knowing what a great fighter Diarmuid is, when you could satisfy Fionn with a handful of berries, though why he doesn't get one of his men to fetch them I can't think."

"Because they're guarded by a giant," Diarmuid explained. "They're special berries that can make an old man young again, but the giant can only be killed by a blow from his own club, which is chained to his body. I doubt if anyone but me could kill him and, rather than have to kill these two to save my own head, I'll get the berries."

So Diarmuid went to Dubros and found the giant sitting beside the tree. He was so big his head was level with the top of it. When he saw Diarmuid he raised his club to strike him dead, but Diarmuid dodged the blow. Then, as the giant lifted it once more, he sprang into the tree and leaped from it onto the club, forcing it down onto the giant's head and killing him. Then he picked berries and gave them to the two swordsmen.

"Take these to Fionn," he told them, "and say you killed the giant yourselves."

This the men did but, as Fionn raised the berries to his mouth, he sniffed.

"I smell Diarmuid's hand off these berries," he exclaimed and shouted to his army to follow him to Dubros.

Now Gráinne thought she and Diarmuid should also eat the berries and soon discovered they were bigger and sweeter on the higher branches. That's why when Fionn and his men arrived, Diarmuid and Gráinne were out of sight up the tree. So Fionn and his men ate the berries on the lower branches and then Fionn sat down to play chess with Oisín. Soon he had Oisín's king trapped so there was only one move that would save him, but Oisín couldn't see it. Then Diarmuid dropped a berry on to the pawn he should move and Oisín played it and won the game. The same thing happened in the second game and the third, till Fionn guessed the berries couldn't be falling by chance.

"This time you're lost, Diarmuid," he cried, ordering his men to climb the tree from all sides.

Thinking them indeed lost, Aengus flew a second time from Newgrange but again Diarmuid refused to be rescued, so that only Gráinne escaped under the invisible cloak. Then, after kicking a few climbers from the branches, Diarmuid again pole-vaulted to safety and followed Aengus and Gráinne to Newgrange.

Still Fionn wouldn't give up, but asked the King of Alba to send a second army to join his in capturing Diarmuid.

"It's crazy," Gráinne said, "for Fionn to make all this fuss over me, when my sister would make him a much better wife."

So Aengus went to see Cormac and Fionn and suddenly all was agreed. Fionn married Cormac's second daughter, promising to forgive Diarmuid, and he and Gráinne lived happily together for sixteen years, rearing four sons and a daughter. Then one night, while they were staying near Sligo, Diarmuid woke to hear the baying of hounds. He wanted to see who could be hunting in the middle of the night, but Gráinne told him he was only dreaming. A second time the sound woke him and again Gráinne said he was imagining things, but the third time it happened he went out and found Fionn on the slopes of Ben Bulben.

"I'm calling off my men," Fionn told him, "for the wild boar we are hunting has already killed thirty of them. Let us go if we don't want to be killed as well."

"I'm not going to run in terror from a pig!" Diarmuid cried angrily, though he knew Gráinne would tell him he should because it had been prophesied that he would be killed by a wild boar. "You go if you wish, but leave me your dog Bran."

Fionn nodded and hurried away but, as he and his men reached the cover of the woods, he whistled to Bran to follow him, leaving Diarmuid to face the charging boar on his own. Then Diarmuid suddenly guessed that Fionn had planned the whole thing in order to trap him.

"Why didn't I listen to Gráinne," he cried, "when she told me to bring my spears?"

With nothing but his drawn sword, he faced the charging boar but the sword snapped in two like a matchstick. Then Diarmuid leaped on the back of the maddened beast, stabbing vainly at his bristly hide with the stump of his sword. The boar plunged this way and that, but couldn't shake Diarmuid off until it charged back up the mountain and crushed Diarmuid's head against the side of a rock. Fatally wounded, Diarmuid fell to the ground but, even as he did so, he plunged the sword stump into the boar's underbelly and killed him.

Fionn, who had watched the whole battle from behind a tree, came over to him then.

"Now," he said, "I have my revenge for Gráinne."

"I never thought the great Fionn could stoop so low," Diarmuid groaned. "Aren't you ashamed? If so, you could still save my life, since water given from the palm of your hands has the power to heal all sickness."

Fionn's men begged him then to save Diarmuid, but Fionn made excuses.

"Where would I find water here?" he asked.

"There's a well not ten yards away," Diarmuid told him.

So Fionn was ashamed to refuse and filled both hands from the well, but, as he carried it to Diarmuid, he thought of Gráinne and let the water drain away through his fingers.

"Must I threaten my own father?" Oisín cried in anger, drawing his sword.

So Fionn filled his hands with water again, but again the sight of Diarmuid reminded him of his hurt pride and he let it drain away into the ground.

Then Oscar too drew his sword.

"I swear I'll even attack my own grandfather," he shouted, so Fionn went a third time to the well.

This time he carried the water to Diarmuid and stooped to give it to him but, before he could put it to his lips, Diarmuid's head fell back lifeless. So he died just as had been foretold, and Gráinne and the Fianna wept for him for many a day.

❧❧❧

# How Niall Became High King
# of Ireland

Another Irish king, Eochaid Mugmedon, had five sons. The four eldest, Brian, Ailill, Fiachra and Fergus, all had rich cloaks to wear and fine thoroughbred horses to ride, but the youngest, Niall, had to make do with a tattered cloak and an old piebald pony. This was because he was not the son of Queen Mongfionn, but of Cairenn, the black curly-haired daughter of the king of the Saxons, for King Eochaid had been her lover.

For this reason the queen hated him. She had even ordered that when he was born he should be left on the mountainside to die and he certainly would have done, for the crows were already gathering about him, had Torna the poet not seen him and driven them away. Now Torna had the gift of second sight and, no sooner had he picked up the crying baby and wrapped his arms close around the child to warm him, than he cried out:

"You are welcome, child, for your future is great. You will be known as Niall of the Nine Hostages and win many famous battles. For twenty-seven years you will rule Ireland and from you shall come a great clan called the O'Neills."

So Torna took the baby home with him and brought him up as his own son. Poets are rarely rich, so he could not give Niall all the expensive toys and clothes his brothers had, but he taught him the arts of music and literature until he could sing and play upon the harp and make poetry almost as well as Torna himself. He also learned the history of his people and how to make wise judgements, as well as the skills of a warrior, so that, by the time he was seventeen, he had all the qualities he would need to become king. Then Torna took the young man to Tara and the men of Ireland called out at the sight of him:

"Surely this lad will one day be our king!"

When she heard this the queen was very angry and said to King Eochaid:

"You have five sons, yet the people would make the youngest your heir. Are you so weak that you will not decide for yourself who is to inherit your crown?"

"There is one wiser than I," the king answered, "and that is Sithchenn the Smith, for he is a great prophet. Let him decide."

So the five boys were sent to the forge on the hill of Tara for the smith to judge between them. When they were all seated in the forge, the smith slipped outside and secretly set fire to the building, shouting:

"The forge is burning! Save what you can from the flames!"

At once Brian ran out carrying the great sledgehammer, followed by Ailill with the chest in which Sithchenn kept his weapons. Fiachra appeared a few seconds later with the bellows in one hand and a bucket of beer in the other, while Fergus brought the stack of wood for reddening the fire. Last of all came Niall, staggering under the weight of the great anvil and its block. Then the smith said to them:

"Brian will be a fine soldier, for he chose the sledgehammer, which must always strike its target. Ailill will be a fine judge, for he chose the weapons of vengeance for wrong-doing. Fiachra will make an excellent scientist, for he chose the blast of the bellows and the ferment of ale, but Fergus will produce nothing of worth, since he chose only a few dry withered sticks. As for Niall, he chose the anvil, the solid foundation on which everything of worth can be forged, so upon his strength and reliability will a kingdom rest."

When the queen heard this she was very angry and said to King Eochaid:

"Will you allow such childish reasoning to decide who will sit on your throne? Let them go hunting and see which of them acquits himself best in the field."

So the five young men went out on the mountainside in search of game. After a while, when they had killed only a brace of hares and a wild goose, a great mist spread over the whole countryside, so that they could see neither the tracks nor the shape of the hills. With no landmark to guide them, they had to stay where they were until the mist lifted. Stumbling over a dead tree branch and feeling hungry, they made a fire from the branch and roasted what they had killed over it. Then they sat down to eat, but they had nothing to drink.

"Who will go in search of water?" asked Brian.

Fergus, always eager to please his older brothers, said he would go. Soon he came to a wood and, following the path which led into it, came upon a well. Delighted, he hurried towards it, when an old woman appeared before him.

"No one takes water from this well without paying toll to me as its guardian," she cried out in a cracked voice.

"What is your charge?" asked Fergus, thinking that he would be glad enough to pay it, draw the water and be gone, for the old woman's grey hair was as coarse as a horse's tail and her teeth crooked, gapped and green as the grass.

"My charge is a kiss," the old woman croaked, leering at him with a grin which showed all her green teeth.

"That I cannot give," cried Fergus, his stomach heaving at the very thought of it.

"Then you'll get no water here!" the old woman snarled.

"I must do without it then," Fergus told her, "for I'd sooner go without than kiss you."

So he went back empty-handed to his brothers.

"I could find no water," he told them.

"Then I must search further afield," Fiachra said, and he set off by the same path that Fergus had followed.

After a while he came to the well and was met by the old woman, just as Fergus had been.

"No one takes water from this well unless he pays me a toll," she told him.

"And what must I pay?" asked Fiachra, edging away from her, for her eyes were yellow and sunk deep into her head, while her nose was as crooked as a thorn tree bent low in a storm.

"The payment is one kiss," she said, sidling up to him in a way he found quite repulsive.

"That's no bargain," cried Fiachra, "nor would I pay such a price for any drink, though it were wine fit for a god."

So he too returned to his brothers empty-handed and saying nothing about the well.

"There was no water anywhere to be found," he told them.

At this Ailill sprang to his feet crying out impatiently:

"What manner of men are my two younger brothers that they cannot find either river or stream? I will return with water if I have to tramp many miles for it!"

Then he set out by the same path through the wood

and after a while came to the well and the old woman. He tried to brush her out of his way, but she dashed the bucket from his hand.

"Wait a while, young man," she cackled. "No one takes water from this well without paying for it."

"Then name your fee," Ailill replied impatiently, for he found the old woman repellent, with ankles as thick as the trunk of a young tree and knees as big as boulders, while her legs were bent inwards under her weight.

"My fee is a kiss from your soft young lips," she said slyly, laying a skinny hand on his.

"I would die of thirst before I would let my lips touch yours!" Ailill shouted angrily and stumped back through the woods to his brothers, never mentioning the well or the old woman.

"Are we to remain parched for a drop of water because not one of you knows enough to find either lough or pool?" demanded Brian, when Ailill reported that he too had failed in his quest. "It seems I must go myself though, as the eldest, it's not I who should be running errands."

So he followed the same route as his three brothers and soon came to the well and the old woman guarding it.

"Stand aside, old woman," Brian commanded, "that I may draw a bucket of water from this well."

"No one draws water from this well without paying its guardian," the old woman snapped.

"Then name your price and I will pay it," Brian ordered loftily, for the skin on the old woman's face was pitted with pock marks and her nails black as coals, so that he was anxious to widen the space that was between them.

"My price is a kiss to be placed on my lips," simpered the old woman, plucking at his cloak with her claw-like hands.

"That price is too high," Brian answered her haughtily as he twitched his cloak from her grasp. "I will have to seek water elsewhere." But instead he returned to his brothers without speaking of the well.

"I have tramped far enough without finding water," he told them curtly. "Let Niall, who is, after all, the youngest and only our half-brother, seek it."

So Niall jumped up readily and ran into the woods till he came to the well. He saw the old woman and greeted her cheerily.

"Good day to you, old woman. Will you let me draw water from your well?"

"Willingly," she answered him, "if you pay the price of it."

"And what is that?" he asked easily.

"A kiss from you on my lips," she told him, holding out her two skinny arms as if to embrace him.

"A kiss is a small price to pay for water if it be fresh and pure," Niall answered and, taking her outstretched arms he pulled her towards him and planted a kiss on her lips.

To his amazement, instead of feeling dry and leathery to the touch, her lips felt soft and moist, so that he cried out in surprise and looked at the woman in his arms. What did he see then but a slim young girl, wearing a purple cloak, clasped at the neck by a silver brooch. Her big green eyes sparkled and her bright red lips smiled at him, showing pearly white teeth, straight and even. The arms he held were softly rounded and the fingers long, slim and white.

"Welcome to the High King of Ireland!" she said softly, and her voice sounded like the rippling of a mountain stream, "for I have chosen you to rule over me."

"But who are you," gasped Niall, "that are so beautiful

now but looked so ugly before?"

"I am Ireland," she told him, her voice now deep as the roar of the river plunging over the mountainside and falling on to the rocks below. "I can be ugly to those who seek to take from me what is mine and destroy it, but beautiful to those who serve me and care for me. So will you find the duties of a king, for kingdoms must sometimes be defended by the ugliness and horrors of war, to prosper at last in the loveliness of peace."

"If I am indeed to be king," Niall said in wonder, "I promise to seek always to keep you beautiful."

"Then take the water from the well to your brothers," she ordered him, "but do not give it to them until they have agreed that you shall be their leader and promised never to fight against you."

So Niall did as she had told him and Brian, Ailill, Fiachra and Fergus swore to honour and obey him always. Then they returned to Tara.

When they arrived, they stood in front of the palace with Niall in the centre and raised their swords high above their heads, so that all the people could see that Niall's sword was raised six inches higher than the others, for everyone knew that this meant he was to be king over them all. So it came to pass that, when Eochaid died, Niall became High King in his place and ruled in Tara from 379 AD to 405 AD, after which his sons, and his sons' sons and his sons' sons' sons ruled for twenty-six generations.

❦❦❦

# Young Siegfried and the Dragon

A cross the sea in the Netherlands, close to the River Rhine, there lived a boy named Siegfried. He worked all day with the man he called his father, though Siegfried knew he was not his real father. His real father had been killed before he was born and Siegfried knew he should think himself lucky to have been adopted by the most famous smith east of the River Rhine.

All the same, he was glad the smith was not his real father. It was not because he was small and stooped with a bald head which seemed too big for his body, especially since his long grey beard reached almost to his knees. Siegfried told himself he could not help looking like a dwarf as he hobbled around his forge and hammered on his great anvil, for he was remarkably strong for one so small. What worried Siegfried about him was the sly expression he sometimes noticed in the small piercing eyes.

On the other hand, the smith told the most exciting stories, all about dragons and hidden treasure. In fact, he talked about such things as if they had all really happened and might happen again at any moment, so that most children would have been frightened. But nothing frightened Siegfried. As he reddened the fire for the smith to temper his metal, Siegfried listened to the stories again and again until he knew them all by heart.

One day, he saw that the smith had made a sword, although no sword had been ordered.

"Why did you make that sword?" he asked.

The smith turned his pale wrinkled face towards Siegfried in a grotesque grin.

"I made it for you," he said, "so you may use it to kill the dragon and win back for me the treasure he's guarding."

Siegfried snatched up the sword, flourishing it over his head and then brought it crashing down on the anvil. At once it shattered into fragments.

"You've destroyed my work!" the smith shouted angrily, but Siegfried only laughed.

"If I could break it so easily, it wouldn't have been strong enough to kill a dragon," he said.

So the smith made another—and another—and another, but every one of them shattered with the force of Siegfried's blows. Finally, the smith went over to a great chest and rummaged about in it for some time. Then he came back holding the pieces of a sword which had a great green agate set into its golden hilt—a sword which had been broken in a dozen places.

"If only these pieces could be welded together," he told Siegfried, "you would have a sword that nothing could break."

"Then how was it broken before?" Siegfried asked.

"By the one who made it: the god Wotan. I've tried again and again to weld it, but I've always failed."

"Let me try," cried Siegfried. "I've been your apprentice ever since I was tall enough to reach the anvil. I should be capable of welding a sword by now."

So Siegfried took the pieces in the tongs and reddened them in the fire. Then he put them on the anvil and hammered and hammered, so that the sparks flew in a fiery arc. He did not stop hammering until all the pieces had been joined together and the great sword lay on the anvil, glittering in the sunlight. Then he seized it and struck it on the anvil with all his might and this time it was the anvil that shattered.

The smith's eyes glinted as brightly as the shining steel.

"Now I know it is you who is meant to kill the dragon," he cried, "for it was foretold that only someone without fear could weld that sword, which is called Balmung, just as only someone without fear could pull it from the ash tree when it was first made."

"And who did that?" asked Siegfried.

"Your father, Siegmund," the smith said. "Your mother brought the broken pieces to me when she brought you."

"My father?" Siegfried cried excitedly. "But why did Wotan break the sword if he made it for him?"

"Because your father angered him by marrying your mother," the smith told him, "so he killed your father and then shattered his sword. But he must have wished you to have it now, or you couldn't have mended it."

"Then take me to the dragon at once," cried Siegfried.

Through the forest of Gnita the smith led him until they came upon a clearing in which stood a great cavern.

"In there," the smith told him, "is the treasure of the Nibelungs, about which I have so often talked to you: sacks of red gold and precious stones, all mined in these mountains, and priceless jewellery, fashioned by me and my brother in our smithy. But no one can claim it because it's guarded by the dragon."

"Then stand back and I'll kill it," Siegfried said casually.

"But beware that he doesn't kill you first!" cried the smith, alarmed at Siegfried's carelessness. "One snap of his terrible jaws would finish you. And even if he misses you with his great teeth, poisonous saliva drips from his mouth. One drop of that will burn you like acid. Then there is his great scaly tail, which he will try to wrap around your body to crush your bones to powder."

"Never mind all that," Siegfried laughed. "The important thing is, where's his heart?"

"Below his left breast, like a man's," came the reply, "for the dragon was once a man, Fafnir, who murdered his own father for this self-same treasure."

Suddenly there came a terrible roar from within the cave, echoing off the walls of rock. The dragon was awake. Without a second's hesitation, the smith fled, leaving Siegfried on his own.

Holding his sword at the ready, Siegfried turned to face the monstrous creature which lurched through the cave mouth, snapping off the boughs of great overhanging trees as if they were twigs. Flames shot from his nostrils and, on seeing Siegfried, he began to lash out with his tail. Dodging away from it, Siegfried snatched up a rock and flung it into the open jaws. The dragon reared up in anger, preparing to pounce upon the boy and seize him in his mouth but, before he could do so, Siegfried thrust Balmung up to the hilt in his exposed breast. With a roar of agony, the great beast hurtled to the ground, flattening the bushes as if they had been heather.

As he pulled the sword from the flesh of the dead dragon, some of its boiling blood spurted on to Siegfried's hand and scalded him. Without thinking, he put his hand to his mouth and licked the sore spot. At once he found he could understand the meaning of the rhythm the woodpecker was tapping out on the back of a nearby tree-stump.

*Siegfried has won the treasures*
*Within the cavern wall,*
*But the Cloak of Darkness and the Ring*
*Are greatest of them all.*

So, when he went into the cave, Siegfried ignored the great sacks piled high with glittering diamonds, emeralds and rubies and the stack of bars of red gold. Instead, he searched until he found the great cloak, hanging from a rock. Beside it, glittering on its bed of stone, he saw the ring. Quickly he slipped it on his finger, flung the cloak around his shoulders and went out into the clearing. There he saw the smith, cautiously examining the dead body of the dragon. In his hand, he held a drinking-horn. Siegfried was about to call out to him when he again heard the woodpecker's tapping.

*Beware of the treacherous Dwarf*
*And his wicked, honeyed lies;*
*He used Siegfried to get the treasure*
*But who drinks his potion dies.*

Siegfried gasped and stayed silent. To his surprise, the smith seemed unaware of his presence. Then Siegfried realised he was wearing the Cloak of Darkness. It had made him invisible. So he stood unseen, watching the smith as he dropped herbs into the liquid in his drinking-horn. The expression on his face was cunning and evil and Siegfried knew why he had never been able to feel affection for him, even though he had looked after him since he was a baby.

"He did it all for this!" he thought. "Somehow he

knew that I was to be the one to kill the dragon and that's
why he reared me! Now he has no further use for me."

He knew then what he must do. Seizing Balmung he
swung it and thrust it into the dwarf's heart. Then he
heard the woodpecker once more, drumming out his
message to the other creatures of the forest.

> *The Dwarf, like the Dragon, is dead,*
> *So the Curse has struck once more,*
> *Therefore let Siegfried take the Cloak*
> *But leave the Hoard on the cavern floor.*

Siegfried took the woodpecker's advice. After all, he
had no need of riches, especially if there was a curse on
them. He was young and strong and brave and now he
even had a Cloak of Darkness as well, so he could be
invisible whenever he needed to be. With these he would
be able to have lots of adventures and find friends with
whom to share them.

ॐ ॐ ॐ

# Thor in the Land of the Giants

F ar away, in the very heart of the Land of the Gods
known as Asgard, there lived a god named Thor. He
was the God of Thunder and he had red hair, a red beard
and beetling red eyebrows. His castle, which was called
Lightning Hall, had five hundred and forty rooms and
was deep in the Valley of Power. Since Asgard was high
above the very centre of the world, which at that time was
called Midgard, Thor was right in the middle of everything
that mattered.

One day he set out in his chariot, drawn by two goats,
Toothgnasher and Toothgrinder, on a journey to Outgard,
the Land of the Giants. He took with him his friend Loki
and, at sunset on the first day of their travels, they
knocked at the door of a farmhouse and asked for a bed
for the night.

"If you are content to sleep on bare boards, as I and my
family do, you are welcome to stay," said the farmer, "but
I am only a poor man with a few acres of mountainy land.
I have no meat in the house to offer you."

"Let your wife put water in the pot and prepare onions
and herbs for a stew," Thor told him, "for I will provide
meat enough for us all."

Then he unharnessed his two goats from the chariot
and killed them both, giving their meat to the farmer's
wife for the pot. Meat was a rare treat for the farmer and

his family and they licked the bones clean. The farmer's son, called Thalfi the Swift because he could run faster than a deer, even secretly split open one of the thighbones to eat the marrow.

When they had finished their meal, Thor told everyone to give him back all the bones and he put them inside the skins of the goats, took up his great hammer called Mullicrusher and waved it over the skins. At once the two goats got to their feet none the worse, but Toothgrinder was lame because his thighbone had been split.

"Was it not enough that I gave you meat?" thundered Thor, the lightning flashing from his blue eyes so that the family trembled with fear. "Which of you was so greedy that he also had to eat the inside of one of the bones?"

"It was I," Thalfi confessed, terrified, "and now I see you must be a god, for how else could you know what I did when I hid it from everyone? Forgive me for my ignorance and I will serve you all the days of my life."

"Very well," Thor agreed. "You shall come with me as my servant to the Land of the Giants."

So, next morning, Thalfi went with Thor and Loki as they set off once more on their travels. After a while, they reached the sea that surrounded Midgard, dividing it from Outgard. Then Thor waved Mullicrusher over both chariot and goats and they rose into the sky, flying above the blue waves until they reached the shore on the far side. There a great forest swept almost to the water's edge and the tree trunks were so thick and so close together that Thor and his companions were forced to leave the goats grazing beside the chariot while they continued on foot.

All day they tramped through the forest, hacking their way through the thick undergrowth with their daggers until they were weary. Then, as dusk fell, they reached an open plain with a great castle set right in the middle of it. It was the biggest castle they had ever seen. So high were its walls that, even though they tipped their heads back until their necks ached, they could not see the battlements on top of them.

"This must surely be the Castle of the King of the Giants," gasped Thalfi.

"We must walk around the walls until we find a door," Thor said.

They walked for a long time before finding a great gate, but it was covered with an iron grille. So strong was it that twenty men could not have lifted it, but it was designed to keep out giants and so the bars were set far enough apart for the three to slip in between them and enter the great hall. There they saw a large company of men seated at two long trestle tables. So large were these men that even Thor, who was the tallest of all the gods of Asgard, found his head barely reached to the level of the tables at which they sat.

"Good night to you, gentlemen," began Thor politely, but the giants took no notice of him, so he struck the giant at the head of the table on the knee to attract his attention.

The King of the Giants, for it was he, merely brushed his knee with his hand as if a fly had tickled him. Thor struck him a second time, using all his strength, but the king merely muttered: "Bother those flies!" though his mutter was louder than a man's shout. Then Thor took Mullicrusher and struck the king's knee with that.

"Did the cat get in?" the king asked his page, "for I'm sure I felt something brush against my knee."

Then, looking down in search of the cat, he finally saw

Thor and his companions.

"Will you look at the three little manikins!" he cried, with a great rumbling laugh.

"I am no manikin!" cried Thor angrily, "but the great god Thor with my friend Loki and my servant Thalfi."

"Oho!" mocked the king. "Then let us see what great things you can do!"

"I bet even my servant can outrun any of your men," Thor told him.

"Then let us see him race against my Wit," replied the king, calling over his page, and they all went outside on to the plain. "The first to complete the circuit of the castle is the winner," the king continued, giving the signal to start.

Thalfi ran faster than the wind, for he was the champion runner of all Midgard, but Wit appeared behind them after circling the castle while they were still watching Thalfi disappearing.

"There is no doubt who is the champion here!" laughed the king. "What can your friend do?"

"I can out-eat all the gods of Asgard!" boasted Loki, so they all went back into the great hall and the king told his servants to set fresh food on the table.

Then Loki was put at one end and a giant called Wild Blaze sat at the other. The king gave the signal to begin and Loki gobbled up all the meat on the wooden dishes in front of him until nothing was left but the bones. When he looked up, however, he saw that Wild Blaze had not only eaten all the meat in front of him, but the bones and the dishes as well.

"There is no doubt who is the champion here!" the king laughed a second time. "What can you do yourself?"

"I can drink a whole hogshead of beer at a single

draught," Thor replied, so the king asked his cupbearer to fill the great drinking-horn.

Thor raised it with both hands and gulped and gulped until his breath failed him, but when he looked into it, it seemed almost as full as before he started.

"We have no champion drinker here!" laughed the king.

Ashamed, Thor went to bed as soon as his hunger had been satisfied and when, next morning, he thanked the king for his hospitality, he added: "though you must think me unworthy of it."

"Since I shall make sure that you never again set foot inside my castle," the king replied, "I will tell you a secret. When you tapped me on the knee, you would have broken my leg if I had not already seen you and taken care to slide an invisible shield of mountains over it and if you look at the mountains you will see the deep valley your hammer made. And when your servant raced he would have beaten any runner except Wit, since my wits are the thoughts in my mind which fly faster than any creature. Moreover, no giant could swallow more food than your friend Loki, but he was competing against Wild Blaze, who is fire, which consumes all things in seconds. As for yourself, the great drinking horn that I gave you was filled from the ocean and who could drink the ocean dry? But you drank so deeply that you caused the sea-level to drop and, in rising again, became the very first wave. So all three of you proved last night that you would be far too dangerous an enemy for me ever to allow inside my castle again."

When he heard this, Thor raised Mullicrusher over his head to strike the king to the ground but, before he could swing the hammer, the king had vanished. Thor and his

companions stood alone in the centre of a vast, empty
plain, for even the castle had completely disappeared.

ఔఔఔ

# Beowulf

B ack in the world of man, there lived a boy named Beowulf, who came of a race of people called the Jutes. In the fifth century, they invaded Britain, settling in Kent, but, in Beowulf's time, they lived only on the northern tip of Jutland, the peninsula in northern Europe which juts up between the North Sea and the Baltic Sea. That part of Jutland is now Denmark but, in Beowulf's day, the Danes lived in the central and southern part and the Jutes in the north.

Beowulf was the grandson of the king and lived in the royal palace. Since he was the son of the king's daughter, however, and had three uncles, no one ever imagined he might one day be offered the throne.

"And isn't it just as well?" his tutor commented sharply, "for you're much too lazy to learn how to rule a country. What's even worse, you're a milksop. No wonder your father left you behind when he ran off to join the Danish king's men. I really don't know how our own king came to have such a useless grandchild!"

As he grew bigger, however, it was discovered that Beowulf had the strength of thirty men in his hands. Indeed, people soon learned to avoid shaking hands with him, for what was only a friendly handclasp to Beowulf could crush the bones in another's hands. For this reason, though he was always so gentle and reluctant to hurt even the smallest of God's creatures that he was looked on with contempt by the Jute warriors, it was decided that he should be trained as a warrior himself.

Then one day something awful happened. Exactly what, Beowulf was never quite sure, because everyone dropped their voices to a whisper as soon as they saw him. All he knew was that his uncles Herebeald and Heathcyn had gone hunting together in the forest and suddenly everyone was wailing and lamenting. Looking out of the palace window, he could see Herebeald, stretched lifeless on a board carried between two servants, and, even at that distance, could hear his Uncle Heathcyn crying out that it had been an accident, a stray arrow, and not his fault. Nevertheless, from that moment everything changed.

The king shut himself up in his apartments and would talk to no one. He could be heard in the middle of the night, wandering about Herebeald's room and crying out in his anguish. He suddenly began to look so old and so frail that Beowulf wasn't really surprised when his tutor called him one day and told him that his grandfather had died.

"If ever a man died from a broken heart, he did," he said. "Now your Uncle Heathcyn is to be king in his place, but your grandfather left you his coat of mail, though I'm sure your cousin Heardred would have appreciated it more."

As it happened, however, he was wrong about this. Beowulf was glad his grandfather had chosen him to wear his armour and was determined to prove himself worthy of it. It wasn't long before he got his chance. One day, not long after his Uncle Heathcyn was killed fighting against the King of Sweden and was replaced on the throne by

Beowulf's youngest uncle Hygelac, a traveller from Denmark arrived at the palace. The news he brought was alarming.

"Soon Denmark will be a country of peasants only," he told the surprised Jutes, "for fifteen of our warriors and nobles are being murdered every day."

"Whoever is committing such an evil deed?" asked Beowulf.

"A monster named Grendel," he was told, "a descendant of Cain who committed the very first murder."

"But why is he doing this?" Beowulf demanded.

"He was woken from sleep by the sound of singing and laughter in the great hall of Heorot, where our warriors were celebrating their victory in battle. Condemned for his evil deed to live alone on the bleak moors, Grendel was enraged to hear others enjoying themselves and he attacked the hall, carrying off fifteen of the king's best men. Not content with that, he returns each night now to seize another fifteen in his great jaws, so that the hall lies silent and desolate."

"And could none of Denmark's warriors slay this monster?" asked Beowulf.

"Many have tried," he was told, "but all have failed and been eaten by this terrible ogre. Though human in shape, he's more than twice the size of a man and ten times as strong. Instead of fingers, he has claws of steel and he will stuff a living man into his mouth and crunch on his bones as you might a hazelnut. Moreover, no sword or spear can penetrate his skin, because of a magic spell that protects him. Who could kill such a creature?"

"I will," said Beowulf calmly.

"You?" laughed the men around him but, although Hygelac told him to have sense, he buckled on his grandfather's chain mail, picked fourteen of the bravest men around to go with him and set sail along the coast for Denmark.

When he reached the court of the Danish king, he was received politely, for his father had been well liked by the Danes, but when he told them why he had come, they welcomed him with open arms.

"God must have sent you!" cried the king, "and if you can indeed rid us of this monster, you will be richly rewarded."

"It's not for rewards I've come," Beowulf told him, "but to save the land that gave refuge to my father when all hands were against him."

Then, excited by his brave words, the king gave a great feast in his honour. The queen herself brought Beowulf wine to drink and, for the first time since Grendel had attacked the hall, laughter and song was heard once more in the land. Then the king rose.

"Beowulf," he said, "although you are not even Danish, I entrust my great hall to you tonight. Go now and rid Denmark of this monster. But I fear you will die like our own heroes."

"If I do," Beowulf told him, taking off his armour and laying it beside his sword, "please send my chain mail back to my Uncle Hygelac, for it was my grandfather's. My body you won't need to attend to for it will undoubtedly have been eaten."

"But will you not wear your chain mail to fight the monster?" cried the king.

Beowulf shook his head.

"Grendel wears no armour, so neither will I," he said. "Since steel cannot harm him, I shall defeat him, God willing, by the strength of my bare hands."

Then he led his men to the great hall and the queen wept to see them go for, like everyone else, she believed she would never see any of them again.

In the hall, the men lay down to sleep, but Beowulf never closed an eye. With beating heart, he kept watch, his ears alert for every sound, but the night was uncannily still. Suddenly there was a loud crash and the great oak door splintered like matchwood as the monster ripped it apart with his claws. Then Beowulf saw this gigantic creature, his eyes flashing fire as he glanced around at the assembled warriors and licked his lips at the thought of feasting on their flesh.

Before he could even disentangle his claws from the broken timber, Beowulf leaped forward, seizing the great arm in his bone-crushing grip, so that the monster let out a howl of agony. He struggled to free his arm from the fingers that shattered his limb, even as he had shattered the great oak door, but Beowulf hung on with all his strength until his whole body shook from the strain and the sweat ran down his forehead. Then, with a sickening crack, the monster's shoulderbone suddenly snapped and, with a terrible howl, he fled, leaving his arm still in Beowulf's grasp.

Now the Danes, woken by the monster's howling, peeped fearfully from their doorways and saw Beowulf, whom they had never expected to see again, hanging the monster's bleeding arm from the gable-end of the hall as a sign of victory. What a cheer went up as everyone hurried from near and far to gaze in wonder at the great arm and the bloody trail left behind by the fleeing monster. Led by Beowulf, they followed it until they reached a bleak patch of moorland, where there stood a dark lake. At the water's edge, the bloody trail ended.

"He must have dived into the lake," Beowulf said, as he saw the waters reddened by the creature's blood. Even as he spoke, dark red bubbles rose to the surface of the lake as more blood gushed upward from the depths below.

"The monster Grendel will trouble you no more," Beowulf told them. "His life's blood has ebbed away."

Then there was great rejoicing and Beowulf was carried in triumph to the Danish king.

"Beowulf," he cried, "you are as much to me now as one of my own sons! I will give such a feast in your honour as Denmark has never known! You shall be given a suit of armour and helmet of gold, a sword with its hilt studded with precious stones and a war-horse with a golden saddle. The warriors who came with you shall each receive a share of gold and about your own neck I now place the greatest treasure we possess: this gold collar."

Everyone cheered and clapped as the king slipped the great golden necklace over his head, but Beowulf only smiled.

"Thank you," he said. "I accept your gifts for the honour of my country and King Hygelac, but you shouldn't thank me. Rather you should thank God, for it was he that gave me the strength of thirty men in my hands so I was able to kill that evil monster."

So Beowulf proved himself worthy both of his grandfather's chain mail and of his royal blood.

❦❦❦

# The Captive Princess

M any years later, on the banks of the River Schelde, where the city of Antwerp now stands, there once lived a girl called Gudrun. She had fair hair and blue eyes and her father was king of a small country which is now a Flemish-speaking part of Belgium.

From the day she first saw him, Gudrun had loved Herwig, the tall, dashing young King of Zeeland, a country just north of her own, which is now a part of the Netherlands. That is why, when Prince Hartmut of Normandy, a kingdom to the west in what is now northern France, called with presents of jewellery and asked her to marry him, she turned him down flat.

Hartmut was hurt and very angry. He thought any girl would be proud to marry the heir to the Norman throne. His father, King Ludwig, was angry too, and his mother, Queen Gerlinde, swore they would have their revenge. Gudrun, however, was very happy because her parents allowed her to become engaged to Herwig and both kingdoms set about preparations for the royal wedding. Then, suddenly, Zeeland was attacked by a dark-skinned race from the south of what is now Spain and King Herwig found himself at war. Immediately Gudrun's father, King Hettel, led his army to help his future son-in-law and Gudrun's brother, Prince Ortwin, went with him, leaving only a small garrison to defend Gudrun and her mother, Queen Hilde, at the castle.

"This is your chance," Queen Gerlinde of Normandy said to her son. "If you still want Gudrun, all you have to do is to go and get her."

So Hartmut and his father, King Ludwig, set sail from Normandy with a large force. They sailed eastward along the coast and up the River Schelde until they could be seen from the castle windows.

"This time Hartmut brings an army instead of jewels," Gudrun's mother cried. "Let us close the gates and get ready to defend the castle."

But the commander of the garrison was a proud man.

"We can fight as well as the Normans," he argued. "They shall die for daring to attack our queen."

So he rode out through the gates at the head of his men, who fought bravely. Even so, they were greatly outnumbered and soon killed. Then the Normans seized everything of value in the castle and set sail for home, taking Gudrun and her serving-women with them as prisoners.

King Herwig heard the dreadful news, just as he was about to celebrate his victory over his attackers. At once, he set off in pursuit, with Gudrun's father, brother and all their men. Crowding on sail, they surprised the Normans, who had camped for the night on a tiny island in the North Sea. A pitched battle was fought but, while Herwig was slaying one after another of the Norman warriors in an attempt to rescue his beloved, Hartmut, Ludwig and a detachment of their most trusted men slipped away in one of their ships under cover of darkness, carrying Gudrun and the other women, their silk kerchiefs tied around their mouths so they could not cry out.

When the sun rose next morning, the beach was

heaped with bodies. Not one Norman was left alive on that island, but though Herwig combed it from end to end, of Gudrun and her women there was no sign. Moreover, King Hettel's body was found amongst the dead. Sadly, Herwig and Ortwin returned home mourning the loss of both Gudrun and her father.

Meanwhile, the ship with Gudrun aboard was approaching the Norman coast. King Ludwig pointed it out to Gudrun, sitting weeping in the stern.

"What have you to cry about?" he asked roughly. "When you are married to my son, all this fair land ahead of us will one day be yours."

"That day will never be," cried Gudrun, "for I will die before I will marry anyone but Herwig."

"Die then," snarled Ludwig, seizing her by her golden hair and preparing to fling her overboard. But Hartmut caught his arm.

"Did we sail so far and fight so costly a battle to capture Gudrun, only to lose her to the waves?" he shouted angrily. "From now on, let no man lay a hand on one who is to be my bride."

But Gudrun seemed not to care that he had saved her life. While the Normans feasted that night, celebrating the success of the king's mission, she sat alone, silent and sad, mourning her father's death and the fact that she might never see Hertwig or her mother and brother again. Seeing this, Queen Gerlinde came over to her.

"Crying won't bring back your father," she said impatiently. "Instead you should be celebrating, for soon you will marry my son and one day you will wear my crown."

"I want neither your son nor your crown," Gudrun told her, "but only to return to those I love."

"Some people don't know when they're well off," the queen snapped. "Maybe a spell living as less fortunate girls do will teach you to sing a different song."

Taking away Gudrun's serving-women, who had been captured with her and become her companions in misfortune, the queen ordered them to spin and weave cloth for the Norman court ladies. Gudrun herself she set to work collecting wood for the fires, fetching water from the well and scrubbing floors. She was given only shabby clothes to wear and left-over scraps to eat, so that she was living like the poorest peasant in her brother's kingdom.

Hartmut might have objected to his mother treating Gudrun like this, but he was away hunting and gaming with the Norman noblemen, while waiting for his mother to win Gudrun's consent to their marriage and, in those days, unmarried women of noble birth spent their time in the queen's service apart from men. Only Hartmut's sister Ortrun was upset at her mother's harsh treatment of Gudrun and sometimes managed to smuggle her a few delicacies from the royal table.

After a few months like this, Gudrun's soft hands, that had never before worked at anything harder than embroidery, became gnarled and rough, and her body grew thin and bony. Then Gerlinde sent for her.

"Now," she said, "you've learned that there are worse things than marriage to a handsome prince who is heir to the crown of Normandy. Promise to marry Hartmut and you may have your serving-women back again and live like a future queen."

"I can't," Gudrun said proudly, "for I am promised to Herwig and nothing you can do will alter the fact."

"We'll see about that!" cried Gerlinde, and ordered that from now Gudrun would do the palace washing.

Now she had to kneel among the barnacle-covered rocks on the beach in the bitter cold of winter with her hands in the icy water, scrubbing the clothes against a board or a smooth rock, till her hands became red and chapped. If the queen managed to find even a speck of dirt left on the clothes she would scream at Gudrun and even strike her, and only Ortrun would praise her when they were spotless and give her soothing ointments for her hands.

All but two of the serving-women cried when they saw their beautiful princess treated like a slave. Hergart didn't cry, though, because she no longer stayed with the other captives or thought of herself as a foreigner in a strange land. She had attracted the attentions of King Ludwig's cupbearer, who promised to marry her and made sure she was better treated than the rest.

Hildeburg didn't cry either. This was not because, like Hergart, she cared less than the others, but because she was too angry. Instead, she shouted:

"Anyone capable of such cruelty deserves cruel treatment herself!"

"How dare you!" raged the queen. "From now on you shall help your mistress until you are sorry you ever opened your mouth!"

So, for seven years, Gudrun and Hildeburg rose at dawn every morning and dragged the heavy baskets full of dirty clothes down to the beach. All day they scrubbed and pounded until the clothes were spotless. Then, at sunset, they dragged the baskets back to the palace. One spring, as snow covered the beach and a thin sheet of ice lay on the water in the shallow rock pools, they saw a small boat heading toward the shore. In it were two men and, as they came closer, Gudrun turned to hide amongst the rocks for shame at her raggedy clothes. Before she could do so, however, the tall man in the stern of the boat called out to her:

"What country is this?"

At the sound of his voice, Gudrun gasped, for she knew at once it was Herwig, even though he was no longer the dashing young prince of seven years ago.

"You are in Normandy," she replied, her heart beating wildly, hoping against hope that he might recognise her voice too, but how could he ever see in this poor, ragged peasant his beautiful golden-haired princess?

"Then perhaps you could give us news of a princess named Gudrun, who was brought here a captive seven years ago?" said the other man, whom Gudrun now recognised as her brother Ortwin, though his shoulders seemed to have broadened and his voice deepened since he had succeeded their father to the throne. "Is she still alive?"

"If you ever set eyes on her you'll remember her," Herwig added, "for she's the most beautiful woman in the world."

At that, Gudrun could hide her feelings no longer, but ran into the water lapping against the side of the boat.

"You've come at last, Herwig," she sobbed and suddenly Herwig saw through the rags and the hollow cheeks and the rough, reddened skin. Leaping from the boat, he flung his arms around her and held her tight, whispering her name over and over again. But Ortwin flushed with anger.

"How dare Hartmut dress his wife in rags and send her out barefoot in the snow to wash his clothes!" he raged.

"I'm not his wife," Gudrun told her brother proudly, "and it's because I refused to marry him that his mother punishes me in this way. And Hildeburg suffers with me because she spoke up for me."

"Then climb into the boat, both of you," cried Herwig, "for our army is camped further down the coast, waiting to attack the palace to rescue you. We came on our own in this way only to find out if you were still there!"

But Gudrun cried: "Am I to leave the rest of my serving-women after me in captivity?"

Then Ortwin kissed her and said proudly:

"You speak bravely, my sister. Besides, no king should steal away secretly something won from him in battle. We will return to the camp and tomorrow we will slay your captors and rescue you and all your women."

So, after Herwig had embraced Gudrun again and again, he climbed back into the boat and rowed away. Gudrun watched the boat disappear around the headland and then, to Hildeburg's amazement, suddenly flung her basket of washing into the sea.

"Now I'm a princess again I will slave no more," she cried proudly.

When they returned to the palace and the queen saw that only Hildeburg had a basket of clean linen, she rounded on Gudrun.

"Where is your washing?" she demanded angrily.

"I threw it away," Gudrun replied carelessly. "I'm a princess, not a washerwoman."

"Insolent girl, I will have you whipped," the queen screamed, but Gudrun only smiled.

"Then your son will have you punished, for I've decided to marry him tomorrow," she said.

Thinking her methods had finally succeeded, the queen sent word to Hartmut, who told the court to prepare the wedding feast. So it was that when, in the cold light of dawn, Ortwin and Herwig's two armies surrounded the palace, the Normans were caught off guard, preparing for feasting, not war. Nevertheless, they fought fiercely, while Gudrun watched anxiously from the battlements. In the end, however, Herwig killed King Ludwig and Hartmut was surrounded. Then Ortrun ran to Gudrun and begged her to save her brother.

"Since you have always been kind to me, I will try," Gudrun told her, so she went to Herwig.

"If you love me, spare the life of Hartmut, for the sake of his sister who is my friend," she said, and Herwig ordered that Hartmut be taken prisoner unharmed.

By now the victorious armies were sacking the palace, killing all who opposed them, and even Gudrun's serving-women crowded around her for protection. Then Gudrun took Ortrun by the hand, saying:

"Stand with me and I will save you from the vengeance of my people."

Hearing this, the queen ran to her as well, begging Gudrun to save her too.

"Why should I help you when you have treated me so cruelly?" Gudrun asked scornfully but, when Ortwin's general burst into the room with drawn sword, crying: "Where is the evil queen who made our princess wash her clothes?" Gudrun looked him straight in the eye and said:

"I don't see her here."

"Then I will kill every Norman woman I find," the general roared and, to save her own life, one of the queen's own serving-women shouted:

"Spare us, for the queen stands here by my side."

"Never again shall you make a slave of my king's sister," the general snarled, cutting off her head.

Then Herwig pushed his way through the crowd and,

flinging aside his sword, took Gudrun in his arms again, so that she wept for happiness.

When, a few days later, they sailed for home, Gudrun took Ortrun with her to her mother's home. Queen Hilde, delighted to have Gudrun back, was glad to welcome anyone who had shown her kindness and treated Ortrun like a second daughter. This she soon became in fact for, when Gudrun married Herwig and went back with him to Zeeland, Ortrun married Ortwin.

Then, for the sake of his bride, on their wedding day Ortwin freed Hartmut, allowing him to return to rule Normandy on condition that he signed a peace treaty with Herwig and himself. As a result, they all lived happily and peacefully for many years.

☙☙☙

# King Gontran and the Treasure

N ot far away, Gontran, King of the Franks, went hunting one day near what is now Luxembourg. He rode for many miles through forests and across valleys, chasing a beautiful deer, but always she managed to give him the slip. Finally the king was exhausted and stopped in a forest clearing to rest. Dismounting from his chestnut mare, he tied her to a tree by her reins while his faithful servant did the same with his horse.

"I will sleep awhile," the king told the servant, "until I get back my strength and energy to continue the chase."

He looked around then for a stone on which to lay his head, but there was none.

"Let me be your pillow, Master," said his servant, for the king was a kind and generous man, whom he had served loyally ever since he was a boy.

So the servant sat down on the ground with his back against an oak tree, while the king stretched out full length upon the ground with his head in his servant's lap and closed his eyes. Soon his mouth parted a little and his deep, regular breathing told the servant that he was asleep. Indeed, if he hadn't been a king, he might even have been said to be snoring!

Sitting watching the sleeping face of his master, the servant was suddenly taken aback to see a little lizard slip from between his master's lips. Too surprised to do more than stare, he watched as it darted across the clearing to where a small stream ran over mosses between high banks. Here the lizard stopped, as if unable either to cross the stream or to go in any other direction. Taking his sword from its scabbard and stretching out as far as he could without moving the lower part of his body, for fear of waking his master, the servant laid the sword across the stream to form a bridge. No sooner had he done so than the lizard darted across it, scurried across the field beyond the forest and, reaching the foot of the mountain beyond, disappeared down a rabbit hole.

The servant sat looking after it in amazement. Could he have dreamed the whole thing, he wondered, but there lay his sword across the stream where he had placed it. Perhaps he had only imagined that the lizard had come out of his master's mouth and it had really come from under the dead leaves at the foot of the oak tree? While he was still considering this, he heard a rustling sound and, looking up, saw the lizard coming back across the field and entering the forest by the same route it had taken before. Hardly daring to breathe, the servant watched it cross the stream once more by means of the sword-bridge, scuttle across the clearing and disappear into his master's mouth.

Hardly had the lizard disappeared than the king stirred and opened his eyes.

"I've had the strangest dream," he said to the servant, "and I would like to tell you about it before I forget it. I dreamed that I crossed a great open space in the middle of the forest until I came to a wide river running through it in a deep chasm. There was no way of crossing it, but I knew that I must not turn either to right or to left. Then suddenly, while I hesitated, not knowing what to do, a great metal bridge appeared before me, spanning the river. By this means I crossed the river and the great plain which lay beyond it until I reached a high mountain."

The servant looked at his master in astonishment, for it was as if the lizard was recounting his journey as it had appeared to him. Before he could say anything, however, the king continued.

"Beneath the mountain I saw a great cavern and into this I plunged. I found myself in a great hallway which led to an enormous room in which I saw, shining brightly, a great treasure. Somehow I knew that it had been buried there long ago by the ancestors of my father, King Clotaire, in order to conceal it from the Huns. But why do you look at me like that with your mouth wide open, as if you had seen a ghost?"

The servant told his master then what he had seen while he slept. At first he spoke hesitantly, fearing his master might be offended, but, when he saw that the king was more excited than alarmed by his story, he hurried to finish the tale.

"And the lizard had barely slipped back into your mouth, Master, when you awoke and began to tell me your dream," he concluded.

"It's a sign from Woden," the king cried eagerly. "He has caused my spirit to leave my body in the form of a lizard while I slept, in order that I may find this treasure, for it was surely hidden so carefully that it might be kept safely from our enemies for me and my children. Let us summon my people to dig in the place where I entered the cavern of my dreams."

So the king and his servant rode back to the palace and, mustering a great force of men armed with spades and axes, returned to the foot of the mountain. Setting the men to dig beside the rabbit hole into which the servant had seen the lizard disappear, the king watched excitedly as the ground gave way under their blows, revealing a passage leading into the very heart of the mountain.

Plunging impatiently into it, the king led the way as confidently as if he had already followed the passage, as indeed in his dream he had, into a chamber hollowed out of the mountainside. Then the men following curiously after him gasped at what they saw. For the chamber was full of warriors' helmets, of a style no longer used, turned upside down so that they served as buckets, and these were piled high with heaps of glittering gold and silver coins. Beside them stood a casket of whalebone, filled with golden buckles, gold and silver pendants and a great gold amulet with the figure of a horse and rider carved in its centre.

So Gontran recovered the lost treasure of King Gundaharius, who was killed by the Huns in 436 AD.

ʊʊʊ

# Roland and Oliver

Long after that, about twelve hundred years ago, there lived a boy called Roland. He was brought up in a royal palace because his uncle was Charles the Great or Charlemagne, King of the Franks, who ruled over what is now France and Germany. One day news reached Charlemagne of an attack on the Italian front, so he set out with his army to repel it.

"I want to go too," Roland cried, but he was told he was much too young to use a sword and was left behind in the fortress of Laon, near Rheims.

Roland waited until everyone else was asleep. Then he took a stout stick, let himself down from a window on a rope, swam the moat, stole a horse from the stables and rode off after the others. When he caught up with them, they were in the middle of a battle against the forces of King Agolant, whose son was at that very moment about to run Charlemagne through with his famous sword Durendal. Surprising him, Roland knocked aside the sword with his stick, saving his uncle's life, and was later rewarded by being knighted and given Durendal for his own sword.

So when, a few years later, Duke Girart, one of Charlemagne's nobles, rebelled and Charlemagne laid siege to his castle at Vienne on the River Rhone, Roland went too. To pass the time during the long boring siege, he used to go hunting, but, one day, his falcon flew straight for the city walls. There it perched beside the most beautiful girl Roland had ever seen. A boy of about his own age, who was with her, hurried over and captured the bird.

"Will you bring back my falcon?" Roland shouted and the boy nodded.

A few minutes later, the drawbridge was lowered and a chestnut mare clattered across it. On its back was the boy, carrying the falcon on his wrist.

"Thank you," Roland said, as the bird was transferred to his own wrist. "I'm Roland, nephew of the Emperor. Who are you?"

"Oliver, nephew of Duke Girart," the boy told him.

"Then we're deadly enemies," Roland cried.

"That's a pity," Oliver replied, "for I and my sister have watched from the battlements as you jousted with the Emperor's men and I've seen few as skilled with sword and lance as you. Were we not enemies, I'd have liked to try my skill against yours."

"And is that your sister watching us now?" Roland asked, glancing up again at the battlements.

"Her name is Aude," Oliver told him, nodding.

"If we weren't enemies," Roland said, "I'd have asked you to introduce me."

"She would have welcomed that," Oliver told him, "for she admires your swordsmanship as much as I do."

"Then salute her for me," Roland said, "and ask her to walk often on the city walls, so I may at least see her sweet face."

Aude blushed when Oliver gave her the message, but she spent more time than ever on the city walls and kept begging her uncle to make peace with the Emperor. Oliver also told the Duke that his complaints were not enough to justify men's deaths on either side, while Roland kept looking up at the battlements and wishing the war between his uncle and hers were at an end. Finally Oliver and Aude between them exhausted the Duke with their pleadings.

"I can't be the first to give in," the Duke protested.

"Then offer to settle the matter by single combat," Oliver suggested. "I'll challenge the Emperor's nephew. If I beat him Charlemagne must withdraw his troops. If I lose, we open the gates to his army."

"Very well," said the Duke, for Oliver had never been beaten by any of his uncle's men and the duke thought he would be more than a match for anyone on the Emperor's side.

So next day Oliver rode over to Charlemagne's camp under a flag of truce and made the challenge. Roland accepted gladly, for though he had no wish to harm Oliver, it would be a way to end the war without loss of honour on either side. Early next morning, therefore, Roland and Oliver faced each other, in full armour, on the small island in the river which served the castle as a moat, while the Duke and Aude stood on the battlements above and the Emperor and his court watched from the river bank. After greeting each other, Roland and Oliver began to fight, their swords striking sparks from each other's shields as they rained well-aimed blows at each other.

Aude watched in agony from above, fearing equally for her brother and for Roland, whose every glance made her heart beat faster, but, so evenly matched were they, it seemed neither could win. Then suddenly, with a great sweep of Durendal, Roland broke Oliver's sword in two, forcing him to his knees. Aude turned pale, expecting to see her brother killed, but Roland dropped Durendal to the ground and smiled up at Aude.

"I don't kill unarmed men," he cried. Then, helping Oliver to his feet, he continued: "Since you no longer have a sword, let's fight with staves."

They pulled two saplings then and fought with them until both were smashed to pieces. Then they began wrestling, trying every grip and throw to force each other to the ground, but again they were too evenly matched and the struggle ended with both falling exhausted to the ground together, locked in each other's arms. By now the sun was high in the sky and their battered armour unbearably hot.

"Let's rest a while," Roland suggested and Oliver agreed thankfully.

They took off their heavy helmets and lay chatting in the shade, sipping the wine and food brought to them, until they felt like old friends on a picnic. Then, in the cool of the evening, another sword was found for Oliver and, helping each other back into their heavy armour, they began fighting once more. They struck blow after blow for over an hour, until Roland began to feel dizzy.

"Can we have a few minutes' truce?" he asked. "My head's spinning."

"Of course," Oliver said, taking off his helmet. Filling it from the river, he dashed the cold water on Roland's face.

"I do wish we were brothers and not enemies," Roland told him then and Oliver agreed.

"If neither of us kills the other," he said, "we could become brothers, for my sister talks of no one but you and there's no one I'd rather see her marry."

Then Roland struggled to his feet and they began fighting again. They were still at it at sunset and, even when it became too dark for Aude to see what was happening, she could hear the sound of their swords clashing. When it became pitch dark they gave up.

"It's not God's will that we should kill each other," Oliver cried. "Let's vow eternal friendship and persuade our uncles to forgive and forget."

Still neither the Emperor nor the Duke would humble himself by being first to give in and the siege continued. Then suddenly messengers arrived with word that the Saracens had poured over the Spanish border with France. Now Charlemagne had a far more serious war on his hands and the Duke realised his grievances were small compared with this new threat. Hastily they patched up their quarrel and joined forces to repel the invasion.

Now at last Roland and Oliver were brothers-in-arms and Roland and Aude's marriage could be arranged. They had a hurried engagement party before Roland and Oliver had to set out for the Spanish border. After much fighting they conquered most of Spain and drove King Marsile and his Saracen army into the mountains above Saragossa. One day Roland and Oliver were playing chess under a pine tree in a garden in Cordoba when envoys arrived from Saragossa carrying olive branches as a sign of peace.

"King Marsile agrees to Spain becoming part of your empire," they told Charlemagne. "Withdraw to France and he will come at Michaelmas to pay tribute."

"Don't trust him!" Roland cried. "When I captured Seville I was offered the same terms, but when I sent two of my best men to negotiate the king's surrender, he cut off their heads. Let's lay siege to Saragossa and put an end to his treachery."

Roland's stepfather, Ganelon, bitterly jealous of his stepson's victories and popularity with the Emperor, jumped to his feet, flinging aside his fur cloak.

"Don"t listen to such reckless rubbish!" he shouted. "Your men have fought a long campaign and want to go home to their families. Why subject them to a long siege when King Marsile has already offered to surrender? I'm not afraid to go to Saragossa to negotiate a peace treaty!"

So, despite Roland's warnings, Ganelon set out for Saragossa and there made King Marsile an offer he couldn"t refuse.

"Of course you could kill me," he said, "as you did Roland's men, but Charlemagne would still take Saragossa, as he took Pamplona, Toledo, Seville and Cordoba. He will always beat you while he has Roland and his invincible sword, Durendal. Kill Roland and you'll have no trouble defeating Charlemagne."

"How can I do that?" asked the king.

"Send me to Charlemagne with valuable presents and twenty hostages. Then he will go back to France, leaving a rearguard of no more than twenty thousand men. I'll make sure Roland is in command. When I send word, you attack with a hundred thousand Saracens. There will be heavy losses on both sides but, when Roland's forces are reduced in number, you attack again with your full army."

"It shall be done," the king told him.

So Ganelon returned to Charlemagne with the twenty hostages and seven hundred camels laden with gold and silver. He also had the secret promise of ten mules of gold for himself if his plan succeeded.

"Here are the keys to the city," Ganelon told Charlemagne, "and hostages whose lives will be forfeit if the king breaks the terms of his surrender. Also I've brought wealth beyond the dreams of princes, so you can return to France at once."

"I still don't trust this king," Roland told his uncle. "I would prefer to face him in battle."

"Then let Roland command the garrison," suggested Ganelon, and Roland immediately agreed, as his wily stepfather had known he would.

So Charlemagne and his army marched away, leaving behind Roland and Oliver, who had volunteered to stay with him. Towards evening Oliver, on look-out duty from a nearby hill, saw the red glow of the setting sun reflected on armour, spread out across the countryside, and hurried back to warn Roland that a great army was approaching.

"We've been betrayed!" he cried. "Blow your horn to warn Charlemagne to turn back, for we are completely outnumbered."

"Am I to cry for help like a baby?" Roland shouted. "Prepare for battle!"

Then he led his men through the pass of Roncevalles on to the great plain to face their attackers. Though outnumbered five to one, they fought with such ferocity that, for every Frank killed, three of the enemy died. Roland and Oliver alone killed more than a dozen between them, before, with the shaft of their lances broken in two and only their swords to defend themselves, they heard the enemy sound the retreat.

"We've beaten them off!" cried Roland in triumph.

"Yes, but at what cost!" Oliver exclaimed.

Then Roland saw that, of his twenty thousand men, less than a hundred were still standing and Oliver himself was wounded. Sadly he was making arrangements for the care of the wounded and the burial of the dead when he heard bugles sounding another attack. This time they were facing seven or eight hundred thousand men and Roland knew even he could not save the day. Too late, he blew the horn, so loudly that Charlemagne heard it more than thirty miles away. Even then Ganelon tried to persuade him it was only the wind sighing in the trees, but this was his undoing. Charlemagne suspected his treachery, had him put in chains and ordered his army back to Roncevalles.

Meanwhile Roland, Oliver and the other survivors were making a last stand at the pass. Snatching lances from the fallen, they fought like tigers until Oliver, weak from loss of blood from his wounds, fell from the saddle. Seeing him fall, Roland spurred his horse to his side and snatched him up in his arms.

"May God keep you, for I must leave you," Oliver whispered and his head fell back, lifeless.

"My dearest friend," Roland cried, "now I wish I'd blown the horn when you first asked me, for then you might have lived!"

Looking up, he saw a group of Saracens coming towards him, but refusing to surrender, he hacked and cut with his sword until he had killed two and put the others to flight. Badly wounded himself now, he dragged himself over to a pine tree and sat with his back propped against it, his sword on his lap. Then his eyes began to close. Thinking him dead, an enemy soldier tried to steal Durendal, but at once Roland recovered consciousness and killed him. Deciding to break his sword, rather than have the enemy capture it after his death, he tried to smash it on a rock but Durendal proved unbreakable, so he put it in a hollow among the roots of the pine and lay down on top of it.

That was how Charlemagne found him, after he had driven Marsile's forces to their deaths in the River Ebro. Even in death, Roland was still guarding his precious sword. He and Oliver were buried together, as close in death as they had been in life, and all France mourned them, but Aude wept most of all.

❧❧❧

# How the Cid Defeated
His Enemies

Some time in the middle of the eleventh century in the little Spanish village of Vivar, just north of the capital of Castile in a rich, vine-growing district, a boy called Rodrigo was born. His father was a knight in the service of King Ferdinand of Castile and, when Rodrigo was only twelve, he showed such skill with his sword that his father took him with him to fight against the King of Navarre, whose kingdom lay just to the west of Vivar.

Three years later, though, his father died, so Rodrigo was given into the care of the king's eldest son, Don Sancho. He, too, was impressed by Rodrigo's swordsmanship and knighted him when he was only seventeen.

"Now," Rodrigo wrote proudly to a friend, "I have my own fine horse with a golden saddle and wear a leather tunic covered in chain mail, with a pointed steel helmet attached to the hood. My horse's bridle is of silver and so are my spurs and the hilt of my sword. I even have my own squire to lead my charger and a train of mules to carry my lance, spare sword and baggage."

He fought for Don Sancho and soon his fame as a swordsman spread. When, during a battle against the King of Aragon, he challenged a count to single combat, the Count's daughter Jimena gasped at his courage and audacity in taking on an experienced soldier so recklessly. Fearful for the life of this handsome lad, she fell so in love with him that, even though his victory caused her father's death, she felt only relief and, soon afterwards, they married.

Then King Ferdinand died and Sancho became King of Castile, giving Rodrigo command of his army, but this promotion and the young general's good looks, popularity and success in battle soon began to arouse jealousy amongst the nobles at court. They could do nothing at the time, since Sancho treated Rodrigo like his own son, but when, six years later, Sancho was murdered and his brother Alphonso became king, they began looking for excuses to make trouble.

One day the new king sent for Rodrigo.

"The King of Seville grows arrogant," he said. "He has seized Cordoba so that he now rules over the richest Moorish kingdom in Spain, yet he has not paid me the tribute due to me as Emperor. I want you to collect this money and bring it to me."

So, taking only a handful of men, Rodrigo set out for Seville. At that very moment, however, it was invaded by the King of Granada, who was anxious to seize some of its wealth for himself. Before Rodrigo could collect the tribute from Seville, therefore, he had first to defeat the invaders. This he did, despite their much greater numbers, winning the respect of the Moors, who called him "Sayyidi," meaning "My Lord" in Arabic. His own men shortened this to "Cid" and, from then on, that was the name by which he was known.

He returned in triumph to Castile, but the jealous courtiers found the opportunity to make trouble.

"He may have brought you great treasure from Seville," they whispered to the king, "but it is nothing compared with the Moorish riches he has kept for himself!"

Now Alphonso had always been uneasy in the company of Rodrigo, who was, after all, Sancho's general, and there was no knowing what he might do if he ever suspected that Alphonso had Sancho murdered in order to get the crown for himself. He was therefore only too glad of an excuse to be rid of him.

"The traitor!" he shouted. "I hereby sentence him to be exiled from my kingdom. Tell him to be gone within nine days or he will die."

When Rodrigo heard this he was shocked, for he had handed over every penny he had collected.

"I swear," he cried, "that I will never shave my beard again until the king has withdrawn this unjust sentence!"

Nevertheless, he and his wife and two small daughters had to leave their home and so, with sad farewells to their friends and neighbours, they rode south towards Toledo, accompanied by sixty of the Cid's loyal followers.

After a while they noticed that the roads they travelled were strangely deserted and that people ran into their houses and bolted the doors as they approached. When, at dusk, they stopped at an inn for the night, they found the doors barred against them and, though they called and hammered loudly on it, no one answered them. After a while a small girl came from around the back.

"Please go away," she said, "for we dare not let you in. The king's messenger has already been here saying that anyone who gives you food or shelter will be thrown into prison and have all his property confiscated. Daddy's sorry but he can do nothing to help you and you could do us a lot of harm by hanging around."

So Rodrigo crossed the river and put up tents on the sandy shore beside it and there they had to spend the night. They would have had nothing to eat, for no one was allowed to sell them food, but a man called Martin from the nearby town sneaked out under cover of darkness to join them, bringing with him as much food as he could carry from his own home. Then Rodrigo said to him:

"You come to join me, but I've no money to pay you, or the rest of my men. Will you help me to get some?"

"Gladly," Martin said, "for the fact that you have none proves your enemies were lying. What must I do?"

"Go secretly to the best moneylenders in town and tell them I cannot exchange my riches for money because the shopkeepers have been forbidden to trade with me. Ask if they will let me pawn my treasure, coming to them under cover of darkness. Also, you must find me two great oak chests covered in leather to look like those a rich man might use to hold his valuables."

So Martin slipped away quietly into the night. After an hour or so he was back with word that the moneylenders were willing to give him a loan. He also brought two splendid-looking leather boxes. Then he and Rodrigo filled them with sand from the river bank and locked and sealed the great bronze clasps. Fording the river so that no one should see the strange procession, for the boxes were so heavy with the damp sand that it took four men to carry each one, Martin led them secretly to the money-lenders' home.

"I could exchange these for a great price in Toledo," Rodrigo told them, "but, as you see, they are too heavy for fast travel and I have only nine days in which to leave Castile. Also men flock to my banner from all sides so I will need four hundred pounds in ready cash to pay them."

"Everyone knows you brought back great wealth from your Moorish campaign," the first moneylender said. "Is that not why the king has banished you?"

"And two great chests of riches should be worth four hundred pounds," said the second, "but we will want the usual interest."

"Whatever is fair I will pay," Rodrigo said, "and when I return I will bring you each a rich Moorish robe with a fur collar. If I do not, you may deduct the price of them from the contents of the chests. Now, quickly, hide them away and let no one know that you have such wealth in safe-keeping for me. Also I must ask you to promise not to open the chests."

"Very well," the moneylenders agreed, for they believed so strongly in the lies they had been told about the Cid that they never doubted the chests were full of pure gold.

So Rodrigo returned to the camp, roused his family and followers and they rode on in the darkness of early morning to the Benedictine Monastery of San Pedro at Cardena. Hurrying to get there before sunrise, they reached it just as the first cocks began to crow.

The great gates were still closed for the night and, as he hammered loudly upon them, Rodrigo was afraid the monks too might not dare to open to him, but the Abbot was certain of his innocence and willing to defy the king's order. The gates swung open and the Abbot welcomed the party, promising to take care of Jimena and the two little girls, Elvira and Sol, until Rodrigo's return. Then, after a great farewell banquet, Rodrigo had to set off once more. The Abbot gave him his blessing, Jimena, Elvira and Sol wept and waved and the great bell of San Pedro tolled as he rode south with his followers, as much food as the monastery could provide and the four hundred pounds.

Rodrigo reached Toledo before the nine days were up

but, instead of stopping there, he went on to Saragossa, where he won so many battles against the Moors and captured so much treasure that, in the end, the King of Castile had to pardon him, thinking it was wiser to have so powerful a man as his friend rather than his enemy. So he restored all Rodrigo's land to him and Jimena, while Elvira and Sol, who by now had quite grown up, he made ladies of the court, where they soon became engaged to noblemen.

Now Rodrigo could shave again, but he had grown fond of his fine beard, so he only trimmed it a little to have it smart and tidy to appear in court. As to the four hundred pounds he had borrowed from the moneylenders, whether he ever repaid the loan with interest and the promised gift of two rich Moorish robes, just to get back two boxes full of nothing but sand, no one seems to know. Maybe he did, for he was an honest as well as a brave man, who always rewarded his soldiers and released his captives, but, if he didn't, maybe it served the moneylenders right for being so ready to believe the malicious lies that had been told about him.

ଽଽଽ

# EUROPEAN MYTHS & TALES

## Other Books by Carolyn Swift

*Irish Myths and Tales for Young People*
*Robbers in the House*
*Robbers in the Hills*
*Robbers in the Town*
*Robbers in the Theatre*
*Robbers on TV*
*Robbers in the Streets*
*Robbers in a Merc*
*Bugsy Goes to Limerick*
*Bugsy Goes to Cork*
*Bugsy Goes to Galway*
*The Secret City*

And for Adults
*Stage by Stage*, Theatre Memoirs